Her

Her

LAURA ZIGMAN

Alfred A. Knopf  *New York* 2002

This Is a Borzoi Book Published by Alfred A. Knopf

Copyright © 2002 by Laura Zigman

www.aaknopf.com

Library of Congress Cataloging-in-Publication Data
Zigman, Laura.
Her / Laura Zigman. — 1st ed.
p.   cm.
ISBN 0-375-41388-X (alk. paper)
1. Triangles (Interpersonal relations) — Fiction. 2. Women graduate students — Fiction.
3. Washington (D.C.) — Fiction. 4. Jealousy — Fiction. I. Title.
PS3576.I39 H47 2002
813'.54 — dc21   2001053985

This novel is a work of fiction. Names, characters, places, and incidents either are the
products of the author's imagination or are used fictitiously. Any resemblance to actual
persons, living or dead, events, or locales is entirely coincidental.

Manufactured in the United States of America
First Edition

FOR BRENDAN

Her

Prologue

She was my fiancé's ex-fiancée; the mother of all exes; my worst nightmare incarnate. Exceeder of all expectations; destroyer of trust; obliterator of reason, rationality, sanity, she was my nemesis, my tormentor, the one I could not get over.

Her name was Adrienne, and I knew she had come to cause trouble.

It didn't take long.

Of French descent (France, not Canada); a graduate of Yale (master's in art history); an avid rock and mountain climber (Kilimanjaro, 1995); horrifyingly gorgeous (more, much more, about that later); and recently single (Francesco, her Spanish painter-boyfriend, had, it seemed, once too often threatened suicide if she refused to marry him), she dropped back into Donald's life, and thus into mine, right before our wedding.

I'll cut to the chase:

I did not handle it well.

I behaved badly; became unhinged; undone, an addict in constant need of a fix.

Given the same set of circumstances, I doubt that many women would, or could, have acted much differently.

At least, that's what I used to tell myself.

It happened quickly:

One minute I was taste-testing cakes, canapés, champagnes; sniffing stationery; fondling tulle (or was it toile?); the next, I was stalking Adrienne. This transition, or transformation, of mine, from bride-to-be to madwoman, was inexplicably seamless, raising all sorts of questions (namely: *Had I always been latently insane?*)

which I was far too busy spying on Adrienne to answer. In almost no time at all, she had become the object of my obsession; the subject of endless speculation, conversation, jealous suspicion; my cross to bear.

Most of the time, when you hear about the other woman in a story like this, she is almost never as ravishing, compelling, beautiful, stunning, elegant, mysterious, sensuous, sinewy, alluring, breathtaking, captivating, insecurity-inducing as you imagine her to be. Most of the time, when you actually lay eyes upon the nemesis in the story (the boyfriend's ex-girlfriend; the husband's ex-wife; their assorted female colleagues, secretaries, upstairs neighbors), she is almost always anything but.

Not Adrienne.

Usually, in reality, in the cold hard light of day, the other woman in a story like this is almost always this: Mousy. Plain. Insignificant. Mildly attractive. Nothing special. No competition.

Upon closer inspection (and several more vodka tonics imbibed in a dark bar where you and your tortured jealous friend are drooling drunkenly over bad snapshots of this unfortunate woman) she will even prove to appear worse: Thick-necked. Thick-thighed. Thick-ankled. Over-nipped. Over-tucked. Over-plucked. Over-tweezed. Insipid. Insufferable. Inbred.

Again, not Adrienne. Imagine this:

Willowy. Exotic. Intoxicating. Dark-haired. Thick-lipped. Big-boobed.

I could go on. And on. And on. And later, I will.

(All this gleaned from a single photograph snatched from one of Donald's albums: the two of them, years earlier, in the Hamptons one soft-lit late August afternoon.)

Get the picture? I did. Immediately. And it wasn't good. And I hadn't even seen her in person. (That's a whole other story, the first time we met. A preview—think push-up bra, skintight T-shirt and jeans, gelatinous lip gloss—her, unfortunately, not me).

So I went a little crazy.

Can you blame me?

1

We were, as it happened, Donald and I, deciding that evening on how we would have our wedding invitations printed—*Engraving? Thermography? Lithography?*—when Adrienne, Donald's ex-fiancée, called to share her good news: she was leaving New York to accept a job in Washington, where we lived, just after the first of the year.

It was late November.

We were planning an April wedding.

And until that instant when the phone rang and Donald ran to the Caller ID box by the desk and froze, I had been planning—perhaps naively, perhaps idiotically—on taking the high road when it came to Adrienne and her relentless pursuit of friendship with Donald. I had vowed, without any true understanding of just how deep-rooted and, well, virulent, my particular strain of jealousy was, I see now, to put an end to my obsession. My suspicion. My frenzied insecurity. I had vowed, as they say, at long last, to get a grip.

On my demons.

On my nemesis.

On her.

Clearly this was wishful thinking on my part; a momentary lapse of delusional optimism (quite common, I'd read, with most brides-to-be), for nothing of the sort—maturity, acceptance, suffering in silence—was in the cards.

Especially now that she—Adrienne—would be living, as it were, in our backyard.

We had been staring intently at three pieces of Crane's Ecruwhite Kid Finish stationery stock that I'd managed to sneak out of Neiman Marcus's sample book as "souvenirs"—the salesman, stout, balding, moist, had excused himself to take a phone call from an important customer: "And will this be a surprise celebration for the Chief Justice?" (This was, after all, Washington.) The three sample invitations were identical except for the method of printing (which is why I had lifted them: to better understand the hefty price differential) and the surely fictional inviters and betrotheds (*Mr. and Mrs. Henry Stewart Evans request the honour of your presence at the marriage of their daughter Katherine Leigh to Mr. Brian Charles Jamison. . . . Mr. and Mrs. Wendell Fields, III, request the honour of your presence at the marriage of their daughter Tiffany Jane to Mr. Phinneas Welch. . . . Our joy will be more complete if you will share in the marriage of our daughter Blah blah blah to Mr. Blah blah blah.*). Running our fingers slowly and carefully over the print on each card; holding them up to the light; sniffing them, even (my suggestion), yielded nothing. We were failures in the study and appreciation of fine printing techniques.

"Okay, I give up," Donald said, throwing the invitation he was holding down onto the table and leaning back in his chair until its joints creaked ominously. "Which is which?"

"Beats me." Neiman's had, I explained, not been kind enough to reward my little theft by providing me the answers on the back of each like a set of helpful flash cards.

Donald brought his chair abruptly forward, sat upright, and yawned passionately. He stretched his arms across the table, pushing the sample invitations aside as he did, and reached for my hands.

"Honey?" he said languidly.

"What?" I said flatly.

"May I speak frankly?"

"Must you?"

Had he ever spoken any other way? Couldn't we, just once, I wondered, get through some task (eating dinner, washing dishes, having sex) without his need to speak frankly?

"Fine. Speak," I said, waving my hand, giving up. Relieved

now to have license to speak his mind (a technicality: he spoke his mind quite freely without my permission, as you'll see), he smiled broadly, then brought his shoulders up in a fake cringe, as if to indicate that he felt just *terrible* about what he was going to say—even though, I knew, he didn't.

"I'm bored," he said, finally, his confession a guilty pleasure (he was a true Catholic, through and through). "I have to be honest, I'm having a hard time caring"—broad smile, shoulders up, fake cringe—"about how the invitations get printed. I mean, why are we doing this?"

I couldn't have been more bored myself, but I wouldn't have admitted it for the world. Instead, I let my mouth sag slightly into a sad pout.

"Doing what?" I asked. "Getting married or discussing the invitations?"

The phone rang.

"Discussing the invitations, of course," he said. He reached to give my hands a reassuring little squeeze but I withheld them for effect. "I *want* to get married."

The phone rang again.

"Because." I was about to explain how costly engraving was compared to the other options and how since we couldn't tell the difference anyway, we could, with a completely clear conscience, opt for the cheapest method of the three—lithography—but I was too distracted by the third ring of the telephone. On the beginning of the fourth ring he rose from the dining room table where we'd been sitting, took three steps over to the desk, leaned across it, turned back to look at me, and cringed—this time for real.

"It's Adrienne."

2

Donald mentioned Adrienne the first time we met. Told me that they were still very good friends. The way realtors will tell you what comes with a house they are selling and what does not. *The refrigerator conveys; the window treatments do not convey.* What he was telling me that day was clear: Adrienne conveyed.

We were on the Delta Shuttle one bleak blustery March afternoon a year ago, coming back from New York, where, coincidentally, we both had once lived, and going to Washington, where, coincidentally, we both now lived.

Never having met anyone worth meeting on the shuttle or the Metroliner but forever wishing I would and forever feeling like a failure for having not (the stories of "women like me" meeting great eligible men while traveling the Northeast Corridor abounded and were legendary. They were also all complete hearsay: I knew no one directly who had achieved this goal. It was always someone who knew someone who knew someone who had met someone. . . .), I assumed the self-defeating posture and demeanor of aggressive disinterest upon boarding the aircraft: sunglasses, completely unnecessary, still on; short black wool peacoat still buttoned beneath Burberry scarf still wrapped; reading material (the *New York Observer*, the *New York Times*, the *New York Post*—having lived in Washington only a year I still, obviously, had separation and identification "issues" with the city I no longer officially called home) at the ready, up against my chest like a shield.

I was coming back from a meeting with my friend Anne, the managing editor of a big commercial book publisher who threw me as much freelance editing work as she could. I had just finished working on *Self-Discovery Through Pain* and was set to pick up *A Gentle Plea for Me: How to Ask for What You Need (Say Please!)*. Needless to say, I felt entitled to a day trip to New York (a little lunch; a little shopping; a gigantic gossip fest with Anne) to offset the journey into self-discovery and self-hatred my excruciatingly painful work was forcing me to make.

As usual on weekday afternoons before five o'clock, the plane was only moderately crowded, so I still had my pick of seats. Fearing death from sitting too close to the front of the plane, too far back in the plane, anywhere near either of the wings, or anywhere in between, I placed half a Xanax on the back of my tongue and swallowed it down with a quick swig of bottled water as I passed behind the cockpit, never breaking stride as I moved down the aisle, waiting for the right seat to make itself known to me. We found each other, finally, my seat and I, some rows down, between the wing and the backmost part of the cabin: row twenty-eight; left; window. I wasn't certain that in the event of an emergency it would be the seat which would save my life: all I knew was that it wasn't exuding a positive death vibe.

In minutes after I had settled in (coat off, scarf draped across my lap, bag stowed beneath the middle seat in front of me, *New York Observer* unfolded, Xanax coursing nicely through my veins) the plane began to fill up. It was 2:45 p.m.—fifteen minutes before our scheduled departure—when an extremely tall man began making his way down the aisle. He ducked the cabin's low ceiling as best he could but failed miserably—slouching, twisting himself this way and that—and as he did I couldn't seem to take my eyes off of him: not for any lustful or lascivious reasons, but because he was making such a spectacle of himself and causing such a scene.

"Excuse me, pardon me, excuse me, pardon me," he said, a mantra which was neither, if truth be told, apologetic nor self-deprecating. On the contrary, he seemed to be rather amused: surely, this was not the first time he had trouble fitting his too-tall too-broad frame down the too-small aisle of a filling airplane, and he clearly derived some sort of comic pleasure out of the ungainly sight and sound of his limbs and briefcase and skull hitting plastic overhead compartments and armrests and seat backs as he moved. I turned back to my newspaper, but before I did, I thought I noticed him heading my way—or, rather, toward the empty aisle seat that was still available to my right.

God, he was cute.

"Excuse me, pardon me, excuse me, pardon me," I heard him mutter again, this time with a low chuckle as he made his way further down the aisle to the back of the cabin. And then, upon stopping at row twenty-eight, he said: "Excuse me, but is this seat taken?"

I looked up and feigned surprise as if I had not been watching his painful progress all along. "No." I motioned graciously with my right hand as if it were my seat to give away, and tried to mask the faint twinge of dread that had crossed my face. Funny and interesting as he had looked coming down the aisle, and great-looking as he was with his dark wavy hair and rimless glasses and big easy smile, he looked like a talker. And while that was what you had to do in order to meet someone—a man—talk—I wasn't so sure now that he was someone I wanted to meet.

"Sorry, I'm sorry. Sorry." He was now maneuvering himself from storing his coat in the overhead bin to hurtling himself into his seat, causing himself to hit the head of the man in front of him and to graze the left cheek of the woman sitting across the aisle. Landing in his seat with a loud thud, storing his briefcase under the same middle seat where I had slid mine, then leaning as far back as possible into the unyielding cushion of the minimally reclining recliner, he closed his eyes and let out a long, low sigh of relief.

"I just had a vision," he said, turning to me with his head still back against the pillow. "I do that again, struggling down the aisle, only this time I'm wearing a suit of armor. Chain mail. Wielding a sword. I slash and burn and pillage my way to my seat in the back of the plane as people cower in fear."

I glanced toward him, smiled politely.

Why couldn't I, just for once, sit next to someone who wasn't a violent medievalist?

"No raping, of course," he added, clarifying. "Just the slashing and burning and pillaging. Deep down, you see, I'm really a pacifist."

Despite myself, I laughed out loud. So did he. The plane backed out of the gate slowly, then turned, nose first, toward the runway.

"God, I hate flying," he said.

"Me, too."

"Fear of dwarfing my surroundings, being accused of gigantism."

I nodded, then added: "Fear of death."

In minutes, we took off, hurtling down the bumpy rutted runway with wings and seats and metal joints creaking; then we were airborne, rising slowly into the sky and awkwardly arcing south. The plane shuddered violently and it occurred to me suddenly that I hadn't moved a muscle or even breathed since we were on the ground at LaGuardia. I would have popped the other half of that Xanax, but the thought only made me more rigid. I waited before even opening my eyes.

It was, technically, a short flight—only fifty-seven minutes in the air, the captain said—and we were nearly ten minutes into it. As the beverage cart approached, the flight attendants dispensed cans of soda and juice, plastic cups of ice and lilliputian foil packets of low-fat pretzel snacks with the poise and pride usually associated with people saving the hungry in famine-racked countries. My seatmate and I resumed our pre-flight conversation.

"So how tall *are* you?" A lame opening gambit, I knew, but at least I was, as they say, trying to "engage."

"Six six."

"My!" I said, my voice seemingly full of wonder and admiration, when, really, what I was thinking was this: *Verging on freak-ish?* Receiving my cranberry juice from the flight attendant I tried to make the sudden images of that infamous eight foot seven inch giant man from the *Guinness Book of World Records* who died too young disappear from my head. Instead, I forced myself to focus on my seatmate's jeans, his olive wool pullover and his sneakers for the first time. Which made me ask him if he always got asked about whether he played basketball.

"Always."

"And did you?"

"Never. I was actually a much better football player than I was a basketball player."

"So is that what you played?"

He shrugged, then smiled broadly, bringing his shoulders up in a cringe position. "May I speak frankly?"

I nodded, expecting more slashing and burning and pillaging fantasies.

"After high school, I never played either sport in college. I was a good enough athlete, but I never had the stomach for it."

"That's right. I almost forgot. You're a pacifist."

He smiled. "No. I'm a chicken! Those guys were huge! I was afraid!"

I sipped my drink and he sipped his (Diet Coke); the plane dipped and climbed, newspapers were folded, refolded. We exchanged names (Elise, Donald), established that we were both flying home, started to talk about what had made each of us leave New York.

"You go first," he said.

"Why me?"

"Because I'm eating." He ripped open a foil packet of pretzel snacks—his third, charmingly extracted from the flight attendant with the finesse of a skilled surgeon or an adorable child. "I'm still growing," he had said, and she had lowered her bag of goodies like a bowl of trick-or-treat candy for him to pick from. So enamored of him and his appetite, it seemed to me, that I was surprised she continued down the aisle without spending some time sitting on his lap with her tongue in his ear.

I thought a minute. "Let's just say I'd had enough."

"Enough of what?"

I didn't want to get into it all—the twice weekly appointments with Dr. Frond, my former psychotherapist; the weekly vitamin drips and injections and biweekly acupuncture tune-ups and constant rotation of therapeutic facials and massages and other stress-reductive health and beauty techniques to holistically treat an angry and disruptive thyroid gland and to try to keep me looking young and hip enough to fit in at the adolescent girls' magazine I worked for: *Sassy*. Not to mention all the failed relationships, the requisite panic attacks that went with them (and appropriate psychopharmaceuticals: Zoloft, Wellbutrin, Paxil, BuSpar, Xanax—individually and in combination cocktail recipes), and the overwhelming sense, every minute of every day (especially during editorial meetings, when "story" ideas were batted around: "Teen Skin: Stop Wrinkles Decades Before They Start"; "Will That Cafeteria Lunch Give You Cellulite?"; "What Do You Really Know About the Boy You're Dating?") that life was passing me by. With a vengeance. Which was why I had left and decided to go to graduate school (Georgetown) and get a master's degree in education in order to do something "worthwhile." So I just said this:

"I had kind of a stressful job."

"Where?"

"At a magazine."

"Which one?"

I folded my hands in my lap, a clear signal that this was my final answer:

"A stupid one, okay?"

"Okay." He seemed surprised by my flash of temper, but not put off by it. Which made me feel ashamed. I hated it when I was nasty and rude for almost no reason (I say almost: the subject of New York and why I left it always made me react as if I'd been provoked to defend my greatest failure, as did facing possible rejection from a man who was a potential date or mate). So I decided to try not to take too much more for granted in this first conversation and be nicer.

"But now I have an easier, more normal life." Meaning: now that I no longer lived in Manhattan, was in school (technically: I was taking a semester off), and worked from home, I had things I'd never had before as an adult. Like, a bedroom. And a car (a 1998 "pre-owned" five-speed Jetta). And time to take long drives.

"What do you do?"

What *did* I do, besides worry about money, and the future, and whether I really wanted to be a teacher or if I'd just used going back to school as an excuse to escape from New York?

"I'm a freelance editor."

Living off the fumes of my ever-dwindling savings account.

"*Really*," he said. He sounded rather impressed. "An editor of what?"

"Books."

"*Really*," he said again. "Fiction or nonfiction?"

"Nonfiction, mostly."

The dregs of it, anyway: beauty, diet, and exercise, all puffed up and masquerading as self-help, self-improvement.

"That must be really interesting." I knew he was thinking politics. History. Lyndon Johnson.

"It is."

It wasn't.

Take the project I was also working on then, for instance: *The Working Woman's Guide to Health and Fitness in the New Millen-*

nium, with its rehashed rehash of sample diets, recipes, exercise regimens—none of which, as far as I could tell, had anything to do with any millennium, let alone the new one.

My life was a farce.

"Actually, it's not interesting."

"Oh."

"A lot of indexing. Fact-checking. Repagination."

Was I trying to repel him or was it just happening by accident?

"And what about you?" I asked, quickly looking to change the subject.

"I worked on Wall Street for almost fifteen years," he started. "Merrill Lynch. Morgan Stanley. Arbitrage, bond trader, hedge fund manager before I left. The money was good but I got tired of working eighteen-hour days and eating pad thai at my desk every night at midnight. I hate pad thai. It's so—" he looked around for a second or two, trying to find the right word—"so *nothing*. Everybody always made such a big deal over pad thai. '*Ooooh, pad thai this and pad thai that!*' But I mean, can I just say? *It's just noodles!*" He paused, took a breath, collected himself. "Anyway, I quit my job, took my money, and moved away. I'm an English teacher now."

"*Really*," I said. What a coincidence. But then I considered the time of day and day of the week we were having this conversation: Weren't schoolteachers supposed to be in school teaching right now? Either he was lying or playing hooky.

"I'm on spring break this week," he said, as if reading my suspicious mind, which, I've been told, isn't that difficult to do: my overarching eyebrow, generalized look of mistrust, disgust are usually dead giveaways.

"Public or private school?"

"Private."

"Which one?"

"I used to be at Sidwell Friends."

"Sure. I've heard of it," I said.

"Chelsea Clinton went there."

"I know."

"Of course you would."

He nodded. "Now I'm at a different school."

I nodded.

"What do you teach?"

"Ninth and tenth grade."

I winced. "Fourteen- and fifteen-year-olds," I said. "Now that's a tough age."

"You have no idea."

"Really."

"They test you, torment you, lie all the time."

I raised an eyebrow. Maybe I should switch to law school.

"For instance, I spent my whole first week refusing to make them hot chocolate in the afternoon."

"Hot chocolate?"

"Hot chocolate. It seems the teacher I had replaced liked to have a little snack time in order to—" he was using his hands quite a bit here, as if to explicate something that was clearly inexplicable.

"Infantilize them?" Having only gone to public schools myself, I doubted I would ever understand the mentality of the private school child.

"Exactly," he said.

"Unbelievable."

"Then, because I refused to serve a hot beverage, a group of parents complained: they felt I was being too hard on their children, and were concerned and afraid that my class wasn't *fun* enough. I mean, sometimes life isn't supposed to be fun." He shook his head, seemingly disgusted. "Anyway, now I bring candy to school—huge bags of those miniature Mr. Goodbars and Krackels and Hershey's Kisses that I buy at Costco. I give them out for reading contests, quizzes, anything. Just so I don't get fired."

He laughed; then I laughed. I loved that he wasn't one of those newfangled adults who went on and on about the wonders and preciousness of extremely badly behaved children.

"I hate them sometimes," he said, and laughed again. "I know you're not supposed to say things like this, but I really do. At least they're better than the fourth graders I used to have," he went on. "Animals. Every last one of them."

"But I thought—"

"You thought because it's a private school that they'd be more civilized?"

I nodded.

"Even the Quakers. Please. Don't get me started."

Okay.

"Not that they're the worst, of course. Catholics," he said. "Now they're the worst."

"Oh."

"I can say that because I'm Catholic."

"Well Jews aren't much better," I offered. "I can say that because I'm Jewish."

"Even though I'm not Jewish, I feel like I am. I think it's because I lived in New York for so long. All that smoked fish. All those bagels." He stopped a minute, out of respect, it seemed, for all the foods long gone. "I mean, can you find a decent bagel in Washington?"

I shook my head. "Don't get *me* started."

"Anyway," he said, picking up where he'd left off before the rant, "it's just that I came to realize that what I wanted most was a house and a yard."

I sniffed, smelled a wife and kids.

"Wife and kids?" I asked, glancing reflexively but to no avail at the ring finger of his left hand (it was in his lap, hidden beneath a still-folded *Wall Street Journal*).

"No. Ex-girlfriend. Ex-fiancée, actually—Adrienne—and dog. She granted me full custody. It was an amicable separation. We're still good friends, in fact."

"Great!" I smiled disingenuously and turned back to my newspaper.

I had little tolerance for men who prided themselves on remaining close to their exes.

And even less tolerance for women with French-sounding names.

He seemed to sense my disapproval and backpedaled. "I mean, it's not like we talk on the phone every day or anything. We're just friendly, you know? We keep in touch. Every few months maybe, she'll call. Or drop me a note. Sometimes I'll email her a picture of the dog."

"That's nice. That's admirable." I tried for a third self-actualizing life-affirming compliment, but I was running out of lies.

"You think?" he said. He seemed relieved by my acceptance of his sensitive-man live-and-let-live "life choices." Men could be such fools.

I cracked a thin sliver of ice between my back teeth. "May I speak frankly now, too?"

He smiled. *"Please."*

"No."

"Really." He looked crushed, disappointed, then waited for me to continue.

We'd begun our initial descent. The plane banked left, then right, then left again. I felt nauseous. Afraid of plunging, wing first, into the Potomac. Or was it the Tidal Basin? The geography of Washington—physical and otherwise—was still not clear to me.

"Look," I said, dismissively, "I don't even know you. It's none of my business whether you maintain an inappropriate or un-healthy closeness with your ex-girlfriend—or ex-fiancée—or not." Frond-speak. Channeled from the great beyond.

What on earth was I talking about?

"It's not inappropriate. Or unhealthy." He looked wounded, confused. In retrospect, of course, this was entirely justified.

"Whatever. It's just really none of my business."

"I don't even know how we got on the subject of her." He sounded frustrated with himself, as if this happened all the time: meeting a complete stranger and having her turn on him in the middle of their first conversation because he was talking about a previous relationship with another woman.

The plane landed, and we, still sitting, collected our belong-ings. Once the cabin doors opened and the line of human bodies started to move, we both rose and slid out of our seats and deplaned wordlessly. On the ramp connecting the aircraft to the terminal, he asked me where I was going.

"Home," I said.

"Where's that?"

"Cleveland Park."

"Really! Where in Cleveland Park?"

"The corner of Cathedral and Connecticut Avenue. Just before the zoo."

He smiled, seemingly delighted. "I'm on Newark. Just off Connecticut. We're neighbors!"

Tongue-tied, I missed a beat, said nothing clever back. Which made me worry suddenly that we were about to walk away from each other, filter into the sea of people in the crowded airport ter-minal, and never meet again. But before that could happen, he turned to me and tapped me on the shoulder.

"Do you want to share a cab?"

Did I want to share a cab?

More than anything else in the world.

And when he dropped me off in front of my building, I agreed (secretly flattered, secretly thrilled that he'd asked me) to meet him for coffee the following week at the National Gallery.

"Three o'clock," I said, repeating his instructions. "Near the huge Calder on the first floor."

"I'll be there," he said, grinning, looking like the kind of man I'd always wished I would someday meet, "hanging from the mobile."

He was not, as promised—or threatened—hanging from the mobile, but rather sitting beneath it when I entered the gallery a few minutes past three. Wearing a navy sport coat, a bright blue shirt, a striped tie, and gray trousers, he looked like an oversized prep-school boy, off campus for the day in the nation's capital. When he saw me he rose and walked toward me. He was smiling and seemed glad to see me, which was surprising. No man in New York had ever seemed glad to see me.

"You showed up," he said, pleased.

"Of course I showed up. Why wouldn't I?"

"I thought you got annoyed with me that day, at the end of the flight. You know, when we somehow started talking about—"

I pretended I'd almost forgotten.

"Her." I waved my hand: *Don't mention it.* "I was just queasy. You know, air sickness."

We walked onto the up escalator and glided to the café, where a host greeted us.

"Well, speaking of *her*," he said, motioning for me to follow the host first to our table, "I hope you don't mind, but I thought it might be nice if she joined us for coffee."

Joking or not, that was three references to *her* before we'd even sat down. I decided to keep counting.

"I'm kidding. She doesn't even live here," he said pulling out my chair for me.

Four.

"She lives in New York."

Five.

"That's far enough away."

I sat. "Far enough away for what?"

He thought a second. "For there to be a healthy distance."

"Distance is relative."

An understatement.

Mars wouldn't be far enough away for a French-sounding overly friendly ex-fiancée to live.

We looked at each other across the table; said nothing. He seemed agitated suddenly, as if he were suffering from a momentary wave of extreme discomfort, and pushed his chair back an inch or two from the table to try to give himself more legroom. His face contorted itself and he shook his head.

"May I speak frankly?" he said.

Hadn't he asked me this on the plane, too?

"Of course," I said.

"I feel like we've gotten off to a bad start again. Like the first time. I don't know why or how this keeps happening, but I wish we could just forget about her and get to know each other."

Six.

I nodded. If nothing else, I admired his directness. And his articulateness. This obsession of his with truth and frankness was really starting to grow on me.

"I mean, that's why we're here, isn't it?" he continued. "Because we met, and we liked each other, and we want to get to know each other."

"You're right."

He paused, his eyes holding my gaze to assess my level of sarcasm (little to nil) and to gauge the likelihood of a barbed comeback (ditto). When he felt certain enough that it was safe for him to proceed, he pushed himself and his chair back to the table and extended his hand.

"I'm Donald," he said.

"I'm Elise," I said.

And we shook.

And I promised myself, then and there, to stop counting for the rest of the day.

Human beings are liars. Who, contrary to popular belief, lie more to themselves than they do to other people.

Or am I just talking about myself?

I may have said I stopped counting Donald's references to Adrienne that day—that one, brief, impossibly magical afternoon when I was, miraculously and inexplicably, temporarily devoid of all cynicism, doubt, pessimism, and negativity (what Donald refers to with equal parts affection and annoyance as my "Quartet of Jewish Gloom and Doom")—those few hours when I managed to suspend my disbelief (he was too tall; I was too hard; we were both too neurotic; life was, in the end, only misery and suffering) long enough to feel that I, too, might someday find a future with someone and be happy.

But, if I may speak frankly, I never did stop.

Not then (he made several—four, to be exact—more references to her before we parted company on the Mall).

And not now (if pushed to hazard a guess, I'd say we're somewhere in the mid- to upper-twenty-thousand range).

But who's counting?

I was.

Constantly.

Day in and day out.

The more our wedding day approached; the more time elapsed between their relationship (his and hers) and our relationship (his and mine); the more I felt that someone (Adrienne) was in the room with us (Donald and me).

And so I counted, silently, to myself, including not only Donald's references but my own as well. Like the ones I just made:

25,501.
25,502.
25,503.
Her.
Her.
Her.

I wish I could say that the early references to Adrienne (twenty through, say, fifty) were the most difficult, and that after those, all subsequent references (fifty-one through twenty-thousand-plus) barely registered and were painless, mere annoyance. But this was not the case.

And why would it be?

Ask the Chinese the theory behind their most beloved form of torture: One drop of water becomes two drops become ten drops become ten thousand drops (or, in my case, twenty thousand drops). Unless you are a follower of Mother Teresa, or Mahatma Gandhi, or the Dalai Lama, and thus truly humanitarian, pacificistic, spiritual—and, on some very real level (let's call a spade a spade here) *dead*—you do not become inured to unrelenting annoyances, aggravations, indignities.

You become increasingly sensitive to them. Obsessed by them. As I did.

Adrienne was my Chinese water torture.

She was the incessant dripping; the unrelenting pelting; my ever-present tormentor. Drop, by drop, by drop; phone call, by phone call, by phone call.

Examples (shortly after that first fateful call telling us of her intentions to move and thus, ruin my life; listened in on from the upstairs extension in my office):

1. "You live in the best neighborhood—Cleveland Park— that's the only area I'm interested in. Is there anything for sale on your street?"

(*Note to self: Cruise the neighborhood first thing in the morning; search and destroy all "For Sale" signs posted.*)

2. "I'm not going to know a soul in town, except for you and a

few people at the museum (the National Gallery; she was to be the new Director of Special Programs, whatever that meant), so I'm going to have to start meeting people, even though, right now, I don't feel up to it. It's just a difficult time for me. I know this is the right move—especially now that Francesco and I are completely finished. But I've been feeling very, you know, vulnerable lately. And fragile."

3. "Speaking of vulnerable and fragile—how has Lucy been doing since you started her on Prozac?"

Lucy. The dog. That fucking dog. Symbol of the past—their shared life; excuse for the present and future—visitation rights, she was my eerily human nonhuman nemesis.

Insinuating herself back into Donald's life, Adrienne thereby insinuated herself into mine, and as a result, Donald and I were, on the subject of her, little by little, at each other's throats.

"Gee, she calls a lot."

He blinked. "You think?"

"Do I think? Of course I think. She's called twice this week already. And it's only Tuesday."

He gesticulated, explicated, mitigated. "She always gets this way when she's anxious. She's scared about the move, and she's scared about being on her own again after the breakup, and she's just trying to connect with someone to reduce her anxiety."

"She's trying to connect with *you*, Donald, her ex-boyfriend."

"That's ridiculous."

"No it isn't."

"Yes it is."

"No. It isn't."

"Elise, please."

"Elise please what? 'Elise please lay off so my ex-fiancée can continue to try to "connect" with me without you interfering?' 'Elise please lay off so I can concentrate on the emotional needs of my ex-fiancée at the expense of the emotional needs of my current fiancée?' 'Elise please lay off because—' "

"You mean everything to me and she means nothing?"

Silenced, I stopped, hands on hips. "Nice try."

"It's the truth."

"Then prove it."

"How?"

"Change our phone number."

So acute became my insecurity that anyone hearing about it would have assumed that she was the bride-to-be whom I, the scorned ex-fiancée, was trying to depose. Which wasn't how it was at all, of course.

I was the reigning incumbent.

I was the one picking out invitations and caterers and table settings and wedding dresses.

I was the one winning.

Whatever that meant.

But that's what everyone (my married friends, my single friends, even my divorced friends) was telling me:

That I'd found the Holy Grail.

A straight, attractive, unambivalent man who loved me and wanted to marry me.

Who cared if I would never be allowed to complain about my life ever again?

And yet I was the one who began behaving like a lunatic.

I was the one who started going through Donald's wallet, pants pockets, shirt pockets, coat pockets, bureau drawers, desk drawers, briefcase, date book, piles of receipts, old files, boxes of correspondence, photo albums, glove compartment, trunk.

I was the one eavesdropping on his phone calls, gaining access to his access codes and passwords, then checking his voicemail messages and email messages.

I was the one sitting up in bed at night, staring at Donald's face as he slept, peacefully, checking for traces (a telltale twitch, a furrowed brow, restless tossing and turning) of infidelity, guilt, second thoughts.

And this was all while Adrienne was still in transit.

By the time she actually moved to Washington, things would get progressively worse.

I would, on occasion (like, every day), chicken-call her house and her office from pay phones around town (to safeguard against the possibility that she, too, had Caller ID).

I would, on occasion (like, once, or twice, or three times a day), drive by her rented house en route to or from the Safeway, the bookstore, the caterer, the florist, the dress alterer, the videographer, the Justice of the Peace, the wedding site at Dumbarton Oaks.

What was I hoping to unearth when I performed these ritualistic obsessive-compulsive pay-phone chicken calls, and these drive-bys, with my sunglasses on, the visor down, and my Burberry scarf wrapped around my face?

Something. Anything. Everything.

I was checking to see if she was there.

If she was home.

If her lights were on.

Which lights were on (*Kitchen? Living room? Bedroom? Or a combination?*).

If her car (*a midnight-blue convertible two-seater Porsche Boxster*) was parked there.

If anyone else's car (*Donald's 1997 black BMW 740IS, perhaps*) was parked there, too.

If her trash had been picked up (*Was she away? On business or pleasure?*).

If her mail had been taken in (*Had she returned?*).

If her newspapers (the *New York Times*, the *Washington Post*, the *Wall Street Journal*) were still on the front steps (*Was she sleeping late? Alone? With someone?*).

If she was engaging in any suspicious activity (*walking, talking, breathing*).

I was developing, as FBI special crime units call it, a profile on Adrienne—tracking her movements, mapping out her daily routine and schedule, piecing together a composite of who she was from the collected puzzle pieces of what she did and where she went and whom she saw. For no apparent reason I was coming apart at the seams, and had I not been so skilled in the secret art of pathological jealousy (years of practice, from high school on, had perfected my techniques), had I not been so adept at engaging in the disorder's aforementioned requisite clandestine activities and behaviors while keeping those clandestine activities and behaviors hidden from my beloved betrothed, Donald would have caught on to me and left me long before we'd made it to the altar.

Not to mention the fact that Adrienne herself could have caught on and reported my surveillance (stalking) to the police and had me legally restrained.

Either way, I was, inexplicably, well down the road to self-destruction. Along which I risked, at the very least, losing all of our pre-bridal deposits and, at the very most, I risked losing Donald: the one man whom I had ever truly loved and who had ever truly loved me.

Not exactly the normal way for a woman, affianced, only months away from her wedding day with the rest of her (presumably) happy life ahead of her, to behave.

Not normal at all.

5

My obsession with Adrienne started long before her phone call that night; long before I met her for the first time; long before she actually came to live in Washington and sucked all the joy out of my life with Donald. In fact, my obsession with Adrienne and attendant illicit snooping could be traced back to the first time I stayed over at Donald's house; the first time I had, as law enforcement officers would say, access and opportunity.

Not to mention motive.

It happened like this:

Donald and I went to bed together; he fell asleep; and in my postcoital wakefulness, I realized I could, with any luck, make a quick sweep of his house and find a photo of this Adrienne without waking him.

I wish I could say that there was a reason such a thought occurred to me at that moment in time—that Donald had uttered Adrienne's name during sex; that he had uttered her name in his sleep; that there was a near-life-size painted portrait of her, *Rebecca*-like, hanging above the fireplace—something, anything, to explain my sudden need to investigate.

But there was not.

I wish I could say that I not only considered the ethical and moral dilemma of snooping through the belongings of a man I respected and with whom I had just been so intimate (and who, for the record, had given me no reason thus far to doubt the veracity of his affections for me or to suspect the existence of affections for her), and that I struggled with that dilemma, trying to stop myself from doing what I knew was wrong.

But I did not.

I could not get out of that bed and into my underwear and Donald's discarded T-shirt fast enough.

In my mind, at the time, you see, I wasn't doing anything wrong.

I wasn't doing anything inappropriate.

I was simply curious. And, like any other normal woman curious about her new boyfriend's ex-girlfriend, I felt entitled to engage in a bit of innocent information gathering.

Innocent information gathering. That's really how I saw it then.

Standing there in the dark, on the threshold of the bedroom doorway, feeling so entitled, I looked back, literally, and figuratively, only once: to make sure Donald was sleeping deeply enough for my escape to go undetected.

He was.

I crept into the hallway and down the stairs, and headed to his study off the living room.

Never having been alone in his house (an adorable wood bungalow with a wraparound front porch to which he'd added on and renovated the year before) for any length of time until that night, I scanned the room: his desk, bookshelves, file cabinets; his laptop computer, briefcase, address book, date book.

So much to discover; so little time.

But first things first: the basics had to be established. I didn't even know Adrienne's last name.

I sat down in Donald's swivel desk chair, pushed forward, settled in. But then, a noise: Lucy, panting, staring at me from the doorway.

Adrienne's dog, here to maul me, preserve and protect the memory of her former mistress, I thought. At the very least, she'll bark, wake Donald, nail me.

I waited for disaster to strike. But Lucy, a twelve-year-old shaggy black Portuguese water dog, didn't lunge or pounce or defend; instead she sniffed, ambled in, collapsed in a heap at my feet. Maybe this would be easier than I'd thought. Maybe she wasn't as big a fan of her former mistress as I'd assumed. Maybe she could tell me where in the room to look for Donald's secret Adrienne-stash.

If only dogs could talk.

I returned to the business at hand: Adrienne's last name. I opened Donald's address book and figured I'd start at the beginning, with "A." And right there, on the first page, was the entry I was looking for:

Adrienne.

I should have known. Men always put their friends in their address books under their first names, not their last names. Despite the lack of a last name for her, there was a home address (52 East 68th Street) and a home phone number, as well as a work phone number.

I checked the desk clock: 12:30 a.m. Too late at night to chicken-call her at home; too risky to call from Donald's phone in case she had Caller ID (didn't everyone now have Caller ID?). I eyed her work number and picked up the phone: now was the perfect time to call. I'd get her voicemail, hear her outgoing message, which, with any luck, would include her last name.

I picked up the phone, dialed the number; glanced down at Lucy (asleep). On the third ring I heard this:

"Hello, you've reached Adrienne Adler, Events Director at the Museum of Modern Art. I'm not able to take your call right now, but leave me a message and I promise to get back to you as soon as possible."

Blinking, heart beating, adrenaline pumping, I clicked the phone off.

Adler. Adler. Adler.

Jewish?

German?

German-Jewish?

Getting that one bit of information—her last name—that one

detail, that one piece of the puzzle, made me hungry for more: I wanted to Google her on the Internet and see what came up, but Donald's computer was off and I wasn't about to turn it on. Since online spying was off limits for now (I'd do that later, when I got home, I knew), I focused on my next order of business: I needed to find that photograph.

But before I could see past the checkbook, sunglasses, and cellular phone bill in the top drawer of his desk, I heard the upstairs toilet flush. And for a split second I panicked:

Donald was awake.

He would catch me in his office, going through his personal belongings.

If I was lucky, he would ask me to explain myself before throwing me out of his house and onto the street.

And what would I say?

That I was spying on his ex-girlfriend?

That I was trying to use ESP on his dog to find out where the big treasure trove of Adrienne memorabilia might be hidden?

Even if Donald didn't immediately figure out what I was looking for (and why would he? He'd given me no just cause for paranoid suspicions), he would know my behavior was bizarre and inappropriate; at the very least, he would think I was looking for money, or valuables, to steal. Without waiting another second to comprehend what that would mean for our relationship (quite simply: the end of it), I jumped out of the chair and over Lucy, ran up the stairs, and explained to him as I lured him back into bed that I'd just gone down to the kitchen to get some water because I was thirsty. Letting himself be seduced, he smiled at me as if he knew what I was up to.

It could have ended then and there, with the address book, and the single instance of calling Adrienne's office, and the single white lie to Donald. After all, Donald had never given me any reason to suspect he was capable of duplicity or infidelity; nothing in his past pointed to such behavior (he'd never been unfaithful to any girlfriend he'd ever had—at least, that's what he'd told me).

But of course, it did not.

It went on. And on. And on.

The following week, under similar circumstances (the cover of darkness, Donald asleep, the dog wetly snoring—in collusion? I liked to think so, anyway—at my feet), I found a torturously incomplete batch of pictures of Lucy with a woman's (Adrienne's, obviously) lean, tan, fit arm and engagement-ring-bejeweled hand around her neck.

The week after that, I found a photo of Donald, Lucy, and Adrienne at the beach ("We Three: Sagaponack, August, 1996" said the notation on the back in handwriting and language I knew were not his).

And then another photo of just Adrienne and Donald, later that same day: same bathing suits (hers: a chocolate brown bikini); same hair (hers: just below the shoulders, dark, wavy; kept back by a thick, brightly colored, retro-striped headband); different pose (theirs: Donald hugging her—huge smile, tan skin, long long legs—from behind).

Night after night I would return to those two photographs, staring at them in the minimal light of Donald's study, pondering the meaning and significance of each and every detail and nuance of Adrienne's apparent appearance (an example: *Her hair seemed longer than mine. Was it really longer, or did it just look longer in the picture? Did Donald prefer women with longer hair? If so, did that mean I should grow mine out an inch or two? Or leave it the way it was as a test to see if he would love me no matter what?* Another: *Her legs were definitely longer than mine. Like, easily, twice as long. Should I just kill myself now? Or wait? Did that mean she and Donald had better sex than he and I did? Or was it just "different"? Could the length of them possibly have been too cumbersome; gotten in the way of things?*). I realize now that I barely gave

Donald a second glance; just a cursory enough look to notice that his skin was smooth and tan; that his hair was shorter (he was, after all, still working on Wall Street at the time); and that he looked thin. And happy.

Very happy.

And why wouldn't he be?

He was engaged to a long-haired long-legged goddess with whom he undoubtedly had fabulous sex and they were at the beach together, writhing around in the sand and posing for the camera.

Let's just say that by the following week, looking for relics of his past life with Adrienne had become my sport and my pastime; a slightly compulsive though innocent (remember: I was still *just curious* then) habit I couldn't quite kick.

And in the beginning, when he and I were getting to know each other and everything between us was new and uncertain; when gathering information on Adrienne was simply a way for me to feel as if I had some control over all that was new and uncertain—over Donald, over the fear that our relationship, like every other one I'd ever had, wouldn't work out—I didn't think I had to kick it. My doubts were, I knew, in this early stage, self-generated. Donald seemed to have no secrets, and nothing to hide when it came to Adrienne.

His desk, his thoughts, his life, were an open book.

6

But back to the beginning.

Donald and I fell in love shortly after that shuttle flight, shortly after the coffee date at the National Gallery, shortly after we'd slept together for the first time, three dinner dates later.

I never usually waited that long—three dates (four dates, total, if you counted the coffee date, which we didn't, since we both felt it was, technically, more exploratory than infatuatory)—to sleep with someone, and I felt heady from the sense of self-discipline and self-control that prolonging the inevitable was giving me.

"Such self-restraint," Anne, my current book-editing project pimp and former *Sassy* colleague, said when I told her my big news: that I'd met someone—on that infernal Northeast Corridor, no less—and that I hadn't slept with him yet. "I'm impressed."

I had called her to renegotiate my delivery date on a manuscript I was working on: *Fat to Fit: 9 ½ Weeks to a Perfect Body*. For once, I was actually trying to turn it in earlier than Anne needed it (in order to get paid sooner); she, for once, was trying to stall me (until the subtitle of the book was set in stone: the current one, it seemed, made too many in-house people worry that images of Mickey Rourke, Kim Basinger, and rolling around blindfolded on the floor in front of an open refrigerator full of whipped cream and strawberries were incompatible with women's current notions of body-sculpting).

"You are?"

"Completely. I probably would have jumped him on the plane. Or on the ramp from the plane to the terminal. Or in the taxi back from the airport."

I bit off, then spit out, a tiny piece of fingernail. What an idiot I was; what a missed opportunity. It wasn't every year that a man that interesting and attractive (and frank) crossed my path.

"But then I'm a slut," Anne continued. "A slut who hasn't had sex in over a year."

"I'm a slut, too, you know."

And I hadn't had sex in over two years.

"Of course you are." Her tone was reassuring, conciliatory, ultimately condescending. "But obviously you're more mature than I am."

"What's that supposed to mean? You're the one who's older than me."

"I was actually trying to pay you a compliment," she said. "You know, like 'you're making healthy relationship choices' and all that horseshit." I heard her light a cigarette, then exhale. "Jesus, you're away from New York for only a year and suddenly you're so *sensitive.*"

I closed my eyes and felt my cheeks redden. I was humiliated by what Washington had done to me—how it had made me lose my edge. I was also having a very strong nicotine fit. Listening to Anne light up over the phone, listening to her inhaling and exhaling, I could almost taste the tar and nicotine on my lips, on my tongue, against my teeth; could almost smell the smoke, see it snake into my mouth and down my throat. I had quit, cold turkey, three months before, and I only hoped this new pressure (three dates; a potential boyfriend) didn't make me backslide.

"I know. It's terrible. I've gotten soft." I stopped short of apologizing, which made me realize all wasn't entirely lost: I was still tough. Maybe too tough. My mind wandered; the camera inside my head pulled back, panned wide: scenes of my being tough on Donald on the shuttle flight back from New York about Adrienne three weeks earlier, and of being tough on him at the coffee shop at the National Gallery, and even being tough on him here and there on our three subsequent dinner dates. I got nervous, suddenly; decided it was time to change my strategy with him: be nice.

"So what's he like?" Anne asked, puffing, inhaling and exhaling.

"He's tall."

"Tall? How tall?"

"Very tall. Six six."

"That's not tall. That's verging on—"

"Freakish. I know."

"But he's cute?"

I plucked a Flair pen off my desk, uncapped it, then stuck the cap in my mouth: Cigarette Substitution Fantasy Disorder. "Very cute. Dark hair. Glasses. Jock-ish build even though he never—" I stopped myself before launching into his whole fear-of-sports-competition thing. Anne would never understand. While she could certainly recognize it, she wasn't particularly interested in self-destructive neurotic behavior. Which is why I decided to try not to mention my discomfort about the existence of Adrienne.

"Even though he never what?"

"Nothing."

"You were going to say something."

"No I wasn't."

"Yes you were." I heard her puffing into the phone suspiciously. "There's something you're not telling me." More puffing. "He's married. Is he married?"

"No, he's not married!"

"Well, what is he then? Gay?" She puffed, coughed, and finally said, under what little breath she had left: "I knew he sounded too good to be true."

"No, he's not gay either."

"So what's the problem?"

"It's nothing really," I gave in. "It's just that there's this old girl-friend. Ex-fiancée, actually. Who he's still friends with."

"Friends with? What kind of friends with? Fuck-buddy friends with?" That's what *Sassy* had called exes who still slept together.

"No! They're not fuck-buddies!"

"Then they're just friend-friends."

"Right."

Friend-friends. That magazine had made morons out of both of us.

"And?" she asked.

"And what? I'm just sort of curious about her."

"Why?"

"Why what?"

"Why are you curious about her?"

Wasn't it obvious? "Because she's his ex."

"Not good enough."

"Of course that's good enough. Every woman is curious about her boyfriend's ex-girlfriend. Not that we're boyfriend-and-girlfriend yet," I was quick to clarify, since we were still, technically, not for much longer I hoped, just friend-friends. "Aren't they?"

Anne was silent. "You want my advice?" she finally said.

"Sure."

"If it ain't broke don't fix it."

I rolled my eyes.

"If it doesn't itch, don't scratch it."

"Okay, I get it."

"Look, Elise," she said. "You got out of *Sassy*. You got out of New York. And now, you've met a great guy. So to celebrate all your good news, I'm going to let you turn in *Fit to Fat* two weeks early."

"*Fat to Fit*."

"Whatever."

Whatever.

"Sounds like you have the world by the balls," she said right before hanging up. "Maybe Washington's not so bad after all."

Maybe she was right. Maybe it wasn't. I paced around my

apartment, then lay prone on the couch for the next four hours, woozy with possibility. A new life. A new career. Donald.

I guess I did have the world by the balls. Only I had no idea what to do with it.

Had Dr. Frond heard me say that, she would have immediately pounced. Eyes and voice and body language trained to betray no visible sign of interest or disinterest (she was a true Freudian), she would, nonetheless, in her mild but unmistakable Eastern European accent (*Berlin? Vienna? Prague?* She would never tell me where she was from, nor divulge any other personal information. Donald, however, after everything I'd told him, began to suspect she was from New Jersey) lead me by the scruff of the neck to my little mess of neurosis and push my nose in it.

This time?

She would have pointed out the often-pointed-out fact that I needed to feel in control of things—thoughts, feelings, situations, people, *men*—that might not, in actuality, or should not, be in my control.

Like Donald and his past.

Donald, for all his eccentricities, for all his idiosyncracies, for all his at times alarming peculiarities—there was his exquisite emotional sensitivity; his obsession with his weight and the compulsive behaviors surrounding the maintenance of it; his extreme dislike of and propensity to become deeply depressed by unseasonably warm weather during winter months; his ability to be completely unhinged by the absurdities and banalities of the everyday world (I'm thinking now of the time we had to leave a restaurant—meal half-eaten, leftovers frantically wrapped up in to-go containers, all because the spinach salad he ordered had several strands of uncooked but bent spaghetti spanning the plate like the St. Louis

Arch)—did not feel the need to control love. He believed in love, trusted in it, knew it would come to him and behave itself if he waited long enough for it.

Which it did, and which I did, sometime after that fourth date of ours.

Looking out that first time through the eye of my perpetual inner storm into his eyes—huge, green, unflinching—I glimpsed:

Inner calm. Peace. Security.

It was dark, though, on the couch, and then in my bedroom, rolling around and ripping each other's clothes off with a ferocity of lust that two years of enforced involuntary celibacy had almost made me forget was possible.

It beckoned; I succumbed.

Later, though, I would see other things in Donald's eyes, too: I would see the ghost of Adrienne lurking around the pupils, hiding beneath the lashes, staring out at me and whispering like a taunting poltergeist out through a television set:

I'm here!

7

Our first real fight was, big surprise, on the eve of Adrienne's first official visit to Washington. It was a mere week after she'd called with her news, and I was, understandably, I thought, still reeling from the announcement, when she called again—this time to say she was coming in for a whirlwind weekend of apartment-hunting and, dot dot dot—and here is where the fight started—anything else we could suggest.

Upon hearing what I later said was an egregiously pushy and manipulative "hint" but what he maintained was "nothing more than an innocent desire on her part to fill up a lonely time away from home," Donald reacted with alarmingly Pavlovian behavior and invited her to have dinner with us. "You must come," he said, then added, as if she needed to be convinced: "I'll cook."

He'd cook?

In the year I'd known Donald, he had barely ever cooked for me. Once, very early in our courtship, he made a plate of perfectly scrambled eggs to replenish our diminished energy following a rather exhausting afternoon on the living room floor. The other time was his assembly of a BLT using bacon he'd microwaved and lettuce and tomato he'd purchased cut, sliced, and washed from the salad bar of Washington's most annoyingly elitist organic supermarket. But he frequently reminded me of how much he detested cooking, and why. When he was growing up his mother, a divorced working parent, had always made him start dinner before she got home from work.

"I refuse to be feminized any more than I already have been," he'd explained, when I suggested he make dinner for us once in a while. After hearing his childhood-based explanation, I had, out of respect for his alleged pain and trauma, never brought it up again.

Until now.

Naturally, upon hearing his offer to cook for his ex-fiancée, knowing he had almost never cooked for me, his current fiancée, I felt betrayed. When he turned to me after hanging up the phone with the upbeat expression of a happy puppy, I stared at him with disbelief.

"You're going to cook," I whispered, more a statement than a question. The blood was running hot beneath my skin, but my face was a sea of calm: white rage.

He froze by the phone and licked his lips. He had a feeling, suddenly, that he was in trouble. Big trouble. But he wasn't certain.

"I thought it would be a nice gesture."

"A nice gesture," I repeated. "And what are you going to cook?"

"I thought I might do a fish. Or a chicken. On the grill."

A fish. Or a chicken. On the grill.

"But we don't have a grill," I said.

"I know," he said, then laughed as if the whole situation—this disastrous dinner waiting to happen; the disastrous timing of Adrienne's move, so close to our getting married—was incredibly amusing. "I guess I'll just have to buy one."

I breathed in, then out. We were less than five months away from our wedding. There were bands to listen to, caterers to test, photographers to meet with. And he thought he might "do" a fish or chicken on a grill we didn't even have. He was a dead man.

"Gas or charcoal?" I asked.

"Excuse me?"

"Gas or charcoal?" I repeated. "This grill you're going to buy."

He looked at me as if he couldn't quite believe what had just happened. Certain I was going to ask him to leave (even though it was, technically, his house that I'd moved into after we'd gotten engaged and that we lived in now) and to take his engagement ring with him (a Tiffany platinum band with small but perfect rectangular baguette diamonds, channel-set, all the way around), now it seemed to him that I wasn't angry at all. The unexpected reprieve caused him such enormous relief that he folded himself into a chair at the table and wiped the flop sweat from his brow with the palm of his hand.

"Charcoal, I think," he said. "I hate the taste of gas."

I nodded. "Actually, I was thinking gas."

"Why?"

"Cleaner," I said, slowly, deliberately. "Easier to clean."

More likely to explode; injure user.

"Okay then. I'll get a gas grill."

"I was thinking, actually," I said slowly, adrenaline pumping; my obsessive need to know as much as possible about Adrienne growing exponentially with every surprising, unplanned word that came out of my mouth. "Maybe I should help her look for a place on Saturday? You know, go with her to a few apartments, point her in the right direction, maybe take her to lunch. I moved here from New York not that long ago, too, and I could help her get her bearings. It might also be a nice gesture."

Donald beamed. "It would be a *very* nice gesture."

I wanted to hit him, then flay him, then slow-cook him on the open flame of that gas grill we were going to get.

"Let me think about it before I definitely commit myself," I said, wanting to leave myself an out in case I had a sudden change of heart (return to sanity). "I've got to go upstairs and check my book, see what the week looks like."

"Oh my God! You're going to meet your fiancé's ex-fiancée!" Gayle said. "Have lunch together—with his approval! How many people actually get to be face to face with their nemeses? To see what they eat?"

I regarded my white Flair pen cap and sucked on it furiously.

Gayle was my best friend in Washington, and I'd called her from our bedroom after leaving Donald downstairs pulling cookbooks from the shelf. Born in London, educated at Cambridge, and, at the age of forty-seven, impossibly thin and childlike, Gayle had the body of a twelve-year-old girl and the sense of wonder about the world (read: emotional immaturity) to match it.

Fascinated by everything and everyone, her erratically "eclectic" career mirrored her extremely brief attention span: over the years, she had been a freelance writer who had contributed feature articles sporadically to the *Washington Post*, *Washingtonian* magazine, and even *Sassy*, which was how we'd met (I'd edited a very funny piece she'd written about growing up flat-chested); she had written grant proposals for nonprofit groups and annual-report copy for think tanks; she'd even penned an as-yet-unpublished biography of Frank Perdue at the behest of a D.C. lobbying firm that had made her an offer too lucrative to refuse (I'd never gotten a straight answer out of her as to why anyone would want to know that much about Frank Perdue). Currently, she was writing for *Congressional Quarterly*, a magazine she confessed she never read and which I confessed I'd never heard of (we were quite a pair; what either of us was doing in Washington I had no idea). Gayle had been through everything—two divorces; four children; countless ill-fated love affairs—though somehow she'd managed to learn nothing from any of it. Every time another dramatic situation befell her—a romance; a breakup; a lawsuit; a career disaster; a terribly disappointing meal—it was as if she had never experienced anything even remotely like it. Unpredictable and unreliable as she sometimes was, and wrong as her instincts and judgments often were about people (and always were about clothes), she was charming and hilarious; completely *sui generis*. Not to mention generous, too—she'd taken extremely good care of me when I'd first moved to town (she took me out for lunch or dinner while I was still in between paychecks; drove me wherever I needed to go before I bought my car; called me late at night when she suspected I might be, and was indeed, lonely; assured me that changing careers, as she had done so many times before, was a sign of strength, not weakness).

I said nothing. The enormity of what I'd just done—suggesting I spend the day with my fiancé's ex because of my deep-rooted, deeply perverse insecurity—was starting to sink in. I was both petrified and excited: I would finally get to see Adrienne for myself. On my turf; on my terms.

Maybe I'd end up liking her, and she'd end up liking me, and we'd end up being friends.

My mind wandered; glided into a fantasy-sequence-dream-montage: Adrienne and me shopping; meeting for drinks; squaring off in a heated intellectual debate at our weekly book club meeting.

Was I crazy?

"You get to see exactly what you're up against," Gayle continued, with her slightly imperious British accent. "What your competition is."

As usual, in her zeal to reassure, she had made it worse—infinitely worse—something I always forgot when I went to Gayle to feel better. "You're supposed to say that I'm not up against her and that she's not my competition, because I'm the one Donald's marrying and she isn't."

"Yes of course," she said. "What I meant was—you see, what I was trying to say was—sometimes we imagine all sorts of things which, in reality, simply don't exist."

"Like thick lips? Big boobs?" And those other willowy intoxicating exotic features?

"Exactly."

"Gayle. I've seen pictures. And believe me, those lips and that bustline weren't mere figments of my overactive imagination. They exist."

"Those pictures you saw were taken years ago, weren't they?"

"Yes."

"By now she's probably an old hag. Fat and saggy with all sorts of stray hairs and protuberances."

"I doubt it."

"At the very best, she's probably completely average and you've just blown her up in your mind."

Maybe. But if I had inflated her (and I truly didn't believe that I had) Donald had certainly provided the air pump and hose. Now there was a Macy's-parade-sized Adrienne-float bobbing around in my head.

"Look. Listen." she said. She always started her important sentences with either "look" or "listen." "We'll take her to lunch. And you'll get to see for yourself who she is and what she's all about. Then you can put your insecurities to rest and concentrate on what's really important."

"And what's that?"

"*Me!*"

We both laughed. Her insistence on inserting herself into my life was one of our favorite jokes.

"No, seriously," she said. "Donald and your wedding. That's what you must focus on. Not this stupid has-been."

She was right, of course. Feeling slightly buoyed by the idea of her support, I whispered, baby-like:

"So you'll come with me?"

"Of course I'm coming!" she said, suddenly breathless, excited. "I'm dying to meet this mythical legendary infamous Adrienne!"

It was after ten when I hung up with Gayle and realized that Donald hadn't come upstairs yet. Creeping toward the stairwell in my stocking feet, making sure to avoid the two floorboards nearest the bathroom (they creaked loudly, I'd learned from my late-night snooping), I craned my neck to listen for sounds coming from below, but all I could hear was an oddly persistent whooshing sound. Making my way down the stairs as slowly and as silently as I could, I craned my neck further and found finally the source of that sound: Donald at the kitchen table, shirtless, stripped down to his striped boxers, flipping through pages and pages of recipes.

As I watched him from my secret vantage point, I remembered how, when I first moved into Donald's house, we used to stay up late every night talking, comparing our previous lives, before we knew each other, in New York, to our current life together in Washington. The superficials always came up short. We were transplants; out of our element; our heartrates and metabolisms and extremely delicate psychological equilibriums still in the process of readjustment. We had the same complaints about Washington (dull food; dull people; a lot of bad shoes and haircuts); we missed the same things about New York (the food; the people; the access to good shoes and haircuts), but were oddly tickled by the occasional "celebrity" sightings our new town afforded us: Tim Russert carrying a pizza box to his car; Cokie Roberts shopping at the Bethesda Safeway; Irving R. Levine making his way through National Airport. Neither of us, though, if given the choice and opportunity, would ever have moved back. Each of us had left to find a better life, and despite the overwhelming and at times excruciating boringness of the place we'd chosen to do it in, we had succeeded. We had found each other; we had moved in together; and now we were on the threshold of setting out on that precarious path into the proverbial darkness: Our Future.

So what if the people around us carried canvas tote bags with public television and radio insignia emblazoned on them and brought their lunches to work in Tupperware containers?

Those nights after we'd talk about New York—the pizza; the

baked goods (it almost always started with food, it seemed); the apartments we'd lived in; the streets we'd loved; the dirt and stress and sense of claustrophobia, both physical and psychological, we'd hated—at my insistence we'd turn on A&E or the Discovery Channel and watch one of those *Raging Planet* shows about tornadoes, avalanches, tidal waves; or a true-crime reenactment program. People ripped from their beds, swept away in mud slides or buried alive in snow; serial killers; men who murdered their families; bodies dug up and then identified, forensically, miraculously, from a single hair, or one remaining fingernail; we'd both fall silent at the parade of human tragedy played out before us.

At first Donald hated those programs, couldn't understand my perverse fascination with them (neither could I, actually). Soon, though, he pointed to my intractable sense of Gloom and Doom as the one obvious answer.

And maybe it was.

Gloom. Doom. Death. Dying.

Dismemberment. Decapitation. Defenestration.

It certainly made sense on the surface.

But though I didn't know it then and could never have articulated it even if I had, in retrospect I think it was just the opposite.

It was like opening a bedroom window on a freezing cold winter night for the sole purpose of feeling warm under the covers.

Curled up on the couch in the dark with Donald watching those shows, listening to the grisly details of each natural disaster, each crime and the criminal who had committed it, I felt safe. Protected. Locked deep inside the nucleus of those moments for me was the furthest thing from negativity and pessimism. It was gratitude—for what I'd found and for what I now had: a home; a life; Donald.

. . .

It was with that suddenly long-lost sense of gratitude that I tried to regard Donald and the situation we were now in, from my spying perch just outside the kitchen.

Staring at the strewn and discarded books and magazines that I'd brought with me when I moved in (though rarely referred to or used: I had my own problems with cooking), I wondered what it was about Julia Child and Martha Stewart and *Gourmet* and *Food & Wine* that was so wrong, so imperfect, so not-special-enough-or-good-enough for our dinner with Adrienne. Tempted to raise the issue—his invitation and what it meant to the future of our relationship and my sanity—I realized what the consequences would be if I did so.

First, we'd be up all night arguing, with Donald pacing dramatically and gesticulating and explicating each sentence of his earlier conversation with Adrienne and then each sentence of our current argument (he had, at one time, briefly considered a career in the theater). All of which would end with him having a complete emotional collapse and pulling his pants down (frustration was only one feeling he expressed through pulling his pants down. Sometimes it was joy. Or annoyance. Or simply to entertain me by catching me off guard: pants down around his ankles, T-shirt stretched over his head like a turban, occasionally with the flourish of a pair of boxers on his head like a chef's toque).

Second, I would demand that he retract his dinner invitation, which would make my offer to take Adrienne apartment-hunting and to lunch moot. I knew he would agree to this by the wee hours of the morning—in order to shut me up and end the fighting.

Third, and perhaps most importantly—perhaps what it was that kept me from opening my big fat mouth and making him feel terrible when in reality, he didn't deserve to (he was just trying to be nice: hoping we could all become friends; trying to inject into the universe the good karma an act of kindness and maturity such

as that could produce. Who was I to deny him that?)—was this:
I would, as any of the zillion relationship self-help books I'd edited
would explain, reveal too much. Insecurity. Paranoia. Neurosis. It
would all come seeping, leaking out. Which would, thereby, cause
me not only to risk complete rejection, but also cause me to relin-
quish too much power: Donald would know then (if he didn't
already) how much Adrienne bothered me, and it would make me
look small-minded and bitchy.

Not to mention the fact that it would also make her even more
of a forbidden pleasure than she already was. Which, if nothing
else, would drive him into her arms.

So I decided for once, for the moment, to keep my mouth
shut, to say nothing of my displeasure about the plans for the weekend. I would be supportive, accommodating, and gracious. I
would help Adrienne in her search for the perfect apartment. I
would take her out for a perfect lunch. I would even shop for Donald's perfect grilled dinner. Taking a deep breath and striding into
the kitchen as if I hadn't been eavesdropping and lurking outside
of it all along, I told Donald to call Adrienne in the morning and
tell her I would meet her shuttle flight at National Airport that Saturday morning and that I would happily be her host for the rest of
the day in our nation's capital.

Hearing this, Donald smiled, then hugged me, then got down
on all fours and pulled his pants down.

I hadn't seen him that happy since I'd agreed to become his
wife.

8

I had only four days to get ready for the big event—my first meeting with Adrienne; the beginning of the end of my life as I knew it. After a cold hard look in the bathroom mirror (clothed; I could never have survived an inspection of my naked body) around three in the morning when I'd gotten up out of bed after tossing and turning most of the night, I knew I could waste not a minute of it.

The following morning after Donald left for work, his briefcase brimming with textbooks and corrected papers and a huge plastic bag of miniature Reese's Peanut Butter Cups and Snickers bars ("I'm afraid the parents will complain and I'll get in trouble if I don't give their children *a choice*," he explained), I called Anne immediately and told her I needed an extension on *The Morning After Love: Getting Past Your Romantic Past.*

"How long?" she asked.

"A week. Maybe two." I tried to be as vague as possible, but she was on to me.

"So I see you got sucked into taking those self-tests."

"What self-tests?"

Clearly, I hadn't even cracked the manuscript.

"The ones in *The Morning of Love.* You know, 'Write down one negative thing about every boyfriend you've ever had,' or 'List the top twenty reasons why you deserve to be loved.'"

I was silent.

"I, of course," she went on, "ended up with completely inverted numbers: twenty negative things about every boyfriend I'd ever had, and only one reason why I deserve to be loved: how accepting and uncritical I am of the men I date!" She belly-laughed; lit a cigarette. I hadn't heard her in such a good mood since she'd been fired from *Sassy.*

"*You* sound happy," I noted, then inquired: "Anything—or any*one*—I should know about?"

She laughed again. "I have a crush."

"On whom?"

"Please," she said, "it's stupid."

"No it isn't. Tell me," I insisted.

"A new guy started in the art department last week. He's so cute I want to kill myself and die. But he's too young for me."

"No he's not."

"Yes he is."

"No. He's not." I was just about to argue with her but she cut me off at the pass.

"And don't give me that feministic shit about older men dating younger women so older women should be able to date younger men. Because it's not true."

"Why not?"

"Because as we both know from our glory days at *Sassy*, at forty-five I'm old enough to be his grandmother."

I laughed.

"I wouldn't get fired for sexual harassment. I'd get fired for being a senior citizen."

I laughed again, but she was right.

"So instead of fantasizing about some boy-child, I'll just keep taking those self-tests in *Morning of Love*."

"It's *The Morning After Love*," I corrected.

"What is?"

"The book title."

"So?"

"So—I just thought you'd want to get it right."

She paused, breathed out loudly. I knew she was pissed.

"*The Morning Before Love, The Morning During Love. The Day After Hate*. You think I care what the title is? I've got more important things to worry about. This is serious business, Elise!

These aren't two-thousand-word pieces for twelve-year-olds about Britney Spears's belly button that can be turned around in an hour! These are idiotic four-hundred-page tomes about relationships and exercise and self-actualization that are 'documented' and 'backed up' and 'scientificized' with indexes and footnotes and bibliographies—all of which has to be copyedited and fact-checked and proofread! It's a pressure cooker here! I'm responsible for getting these piece-of-shit books published *on time*! I mean, God forbid the world should have to survive another two weeks without *Love in the Morning*."

We both laughed; then Anne, calming down, sighed deeply.

"Oy. I gave up a highly prestigious and lucrative career in Scandinavian literature for this, you know," she said, starting the rant that had become all too familiar in times of extreme stress at *Sassy*. I could just see her at her desk, with her head in her hands, dwarfed by piles and piles of paper.

"I know."

"I double-majored in comp lit and history at Vassar for this? I could have been an untenured adjunct professor at some community college by now."

"I know."

She laughed again. "I know you know, Miss I-Graduated-from-Barnard-but-I-Edit-Idiotic-Self-Help-Books."

I let out a long sigh.

"Don't sound so defeated. At least you're in school now. Or on a break from school anyway. You're trying to better yourself."

"Look, I'm sorry about asking for an extension," I said, unwittingly acting the part of a student. "It's just that it's kind of an emergency."

She stopped to think for a second or two. She may have had a stupid job, but she was no fool. "This has something to do with that ex-girlfriend situation, doesn't it?"

I didn't answer.

"You fixed what wasn't broke. You scratched what didn't itch."

"Anne, she's moving here. From New York. In two months."

"So?"

"So I'm going to meet her for the first time on Saturday. And I only have"—I looked at my watch frantically—"a hundred and twenty hours to get ready."

She gave me a month.

I scheduled two half-days of beauty (manicure; pedicure; eyebrow shaping and tweezing one day; haircut and color the next) at the Jacques Dessanges salon in Chevy Chase even though I was, especially now, the biggest Francophobe around. But the French know beauty. And for that measure of certainty—to ensure that the beautification techniques used on me were at least as sophisticated as those used on Adrienne (she had that French-sounding name, don't forget, and got her treatments in Manhattan, which, as I'd once known personally, is the grooming capital of the world)—I was willing to—and did—suffer anything.

Once the basics were taken care of (two days used, two days left) it was on to clothing: What to wear. So important, so impossible to solve was this question (not only did I have to figure out the exact particulars of how I would dress and whether or not I'd have to buy anything, but I had to ask myself and answer far bigger existential questions: What look was I trying to achieve? What was I trying to prove? What did it all mean?) that I decided to put it temporarily on hold and move on.

Considering that it was far too late in the game to truly change parts of my body (my too-big nose; the seemingly substantial fat stores in chins and thighs and stomach folds, which, in reality, probably didn't exist, since I'd been weight-training feverishly for the past six months to get ready for the wedding), I focused on what I could possibly alter in the one-hour Pilates class I had scheduled for

Thursday morning: height. Upon realizing that my trainer, Cynthia, could, at the very least, help me appear taller by stretching out my "spinal ver-tee-bras" and "ab-dominoes" (she was from Mississippi), I felt a blush of hopefulness. When Donald got home Wednesday evening I cornered him in the kitchen and asked him—without telling him why I wanted to know—exactly how tall Adrienne was.

"Gee." He blinked, then tilted his head. "I'm not sure."

Nice try. "Come on. You lived with her for two years. You were going to marry her. You have to know how tall she is."

He blinked again. "No really. I don't think I do."

"Guess."

"I can't."

"Estimate."

He shook his head, an impossible task. "Really, I can't. I'm terrible at this kind of thing."

I pressed on. Cynthia's class was less than twelve hours away and I had to tell her how much to torture me. "You've lived with me for six months! You're going to marry me! How tall am I?"

He smiled nervously, then eyed me up and down, as if he were looking at me for the first time. You'd think I'd asked him to guess my weight again (we'd played that game, stupidly, once—and only once. He'd guessed 142, and while I was, thank God, below that mark, hovering somewhere around 130, I never forgave him for being so wrong). I knew he was trying to figure out what I wanted him to say—did I want him to err on the high side (tall) or low side (short)?—and finally, after a few seconds of testing the waters (and prolonging the inevitable), he took a deep breath and stuck his toe in.

"I'd say you are—well, if I had to make a wild stab, which clearly you're forcing me to do, and which you know I hate—I'd put you somewhere around"—another breath, another few seconds—"five foot three."

My blood pressure ballooned. "And Adrienne?"

"And Adrienne was—" He looked up, down, all around the room. "She was probably somewhere around, oh, five six. Five seven, maybe." He paused again, deep in thought, unwittingly about to make it much much worse. "Five eight at the very most." Upon releasing these guesses into the ether, he braced himself, awaited my reaction.

Nothing.

He shifted nervously. "How'd I do?"

"Badly," I said flatly.

"Shit. How badly?"

"Very badly. Extremely badly. Unforgivably badly."

"Shit."

"I mean, I guess in your mind I'm this short fat blob. Unlike Adrienne who has this tall willowy"—I used my hands here to pantomime with aggressive exaggeration a gigantic elastic band stretching and stretching—"*attenuated* body. Why are you even bothering to marry me if I'm so short and fat and blob-like?"

"I knew this would happen," he said, scowling. "I swore, after the weight-guessing fiasco, that I would never, ever fall for that trick again. And I just fell for that trick again. Shit. Shit. Shit."

Shit was right.

"Was she a dancer?"

He sighed loudly, deeply bothered. "No, Adrienne was never a dancer."

"Are you sure?"

"Of course I'm sure."

"Because I could have sworn you told me she had been a dancer."

He shrugged.

"Well that's a shame. Given her height and body structure, I'm sure she could have had a brilliant career *in the dance*."

He threw his coat, his briefcase, his stainless steel travel coffee mug down onto the table, then slumped into a chair. This is not exactly what he'd felt like coming home to after *shtupping* ninth graders with candy all day, I knew, and I was sorry I'd started the whole thing. But I was in deep now, and I couldn't stop to save my life.

"How far off was I?" he asked miserably.

I looked up at the ceiling, picked at a cuticle, tapped my foot. "Far enough." I was five four. And a half. There was a world of difference—and a world of hurt—between that and five foot three. But seeing Donald's face fall out of frustration, out of anger and annoyance at his own ignorance ("Of course I should know how tall you are! What if you were in a plane crash and I had to identify your body?"), I felt a sudden wave of compassion and decided to call off the dogs.

"Never mind," I said. "Let's just," and I sighed here for effect, "move on."

"Are you sure?" he said, getting up from the table and approaching me gingerly, an animal afraid of a spring-loaded trap.

Still too fragile to speak, I could only nod.

"I mean, do you really think you're ready to *surrender to* and *embrace forgiveness*, to *achieve closure* on this *emotionally painful experience*?" He put his arms around me, a giant human self-help audio book, suffocating me with the New Age Recovery Movement platitudes we'd make fun of together, sometimes, when he'd come in to my study and see me—crouched over, pencils at the ready—looking far too serious for the task at hand. "Are you certain you *feel comfortable* about *reclaiming your spiritual and emotional positivity* and *moving on*?"

He bent down and I buried my face into his neck and shoulder. The collar of his shirt smelled like shaving cream and chocolate.

And then we indeed moved on.

Up the stairs.

And into bed.

9

Feeling attenuated after my high-priced stretching class (I mean, what is Pilates, really?) the next morning, and as tall as I probably ever would be, I decided it was time to face what I had avoided all week: the question of what to wear.

Briefly considering—and rejecting—a one-day round-trip to New York to go to Barneys (it was too far; the shuttle fare and whatever I would buy too expensive; the whole idea too neurotically indulgent), I resigned myself to the shopping options in the greater Washington area. They weren't many. Convinced I would find nothing suitably competitive with whatever Adrienne would be wearing (chic, sophisticated, black) at Saks, or Neiman's, or Nordstrom, or Talbots, or (yuck of yucks) Ann Taylor, I went instead to the one store that was as good (and expensive) as any in New York: Embellish.

Fran, the owner, who grew up in the tony suburb of Wellesley, Massachusetts, but sounded as if she came from the streets of South Boston, was a genius when it came to clothes (fit, fabric, sense of style) and people (assholes, asswipes, everything in between). And in the year I'd been visiting her store, looking often, buying infrequently, she'd decided, somewhat reluctantly I think, to become my friend—partly because I wore her down, coming in every few weeks and fawning over all the clothes and her impeccable taste the way I did since it reminded me so much of Manhattan; and partly because I plied her with all the big best-selling trashy novels Anne sent me for free, which Fran wasn't at all embarrassed to admit she loved. Friend or not, though, neither she, nor a visit to her store, was for the fainthearted: with her mane of tight blond curls, her heavy tough-girl accent, and her been-there-done-that-and-it-wasn't-very-good-anyway attitude, she was, always, brutally and painfully honest.

Having suffered, and survived, my two half-days of beauty with the French, however, I figured I could handle Fran.

And even if I couldn't, at this point I had no choice.

"Well, look what the cat dragged in," she said, when I walked into the store Friday morning, seconds after she'd opened. Her coat (subtly aged brown leather, belted, perfect) was still on and she was on her way back outside to have three cigarettes (Merit) and her cup of coffee (double skinny latte).

"I have an emergency," I said, heavy on the melodrama. "A fashion emergency."

She looked me up and down, from my white thermal-underwear shirt and old chinos to my favorite brown hiking boots. "Obviously. You look terrible."

I looked down at myself, avoiding the mirrors. Never, in a million years, would I have worn any of these clothes in New York.

"I know," I said. "That's why I'm here. I need something to wear."

She waved her hand: Go on, go on.

So on and on I went—explaining to her about Donald and Adrienne, about what I was up against, even about my attenuation session that morning. "I might be a different size than I usually am," I said, by way of explanation. "You know, taller."

She stared at me for a second and a half too long, pitched her cigarette across the sidewalk, then turned and went inside her store, located in the heart of high-end retail real estate, suburban Chevy Chase. The little customer-warning bell went off once, then twice, as I followed right behind.

She sat down on a stool at her desk; Olive, her French bull-dog, was at her feet.

"What kind of look do you want?"

I cocked my head. "What do you mean?"

"I mean, what do you want your clothes to say?"

I had no idea.

"Like, do you want your clothes to say, 'Fuck you, Adrienne'? Or do you want your clothes to say something more subtle, like, 'I'm an asswipe for offering to take you, my fiancé's ex-fiancée, around my city to help you look for an apartment when I'm basically jealous of you and hate your guts'?"

"I'm not an asswipe. I'm trying to have a little control over the situation. Operate from a position of strength, not weakness." Dr. Frond certainly would have had a field day with this particular instance of my "situational need for control."

"Like in *The Godfather*? 'Keep your friends close, and your enemies closer'?"

"Exactly." Finally, my mission had been articulated.

"I see your point, but I'm not sure you're tough enough to handle that kind of game."

I swallowed. This was going worse than I'd thought it would. Seeing my discomfort, she softened her approach. Slightly.

"This Adrienne," she said. "Is she really that gorgeous?"

I shrugged, as if it didn't matter, though as we both knew, it did. Much too much. "Of course."

She got up, went to the racks, and started in on me.

"Here," she said, opening the deep purple velvet curtain to my dressing room. "Put this [diaphanous Dries Van Noten silk blouse, long slim black wool Dries Van Noten skirt, Robert Clergerie boots] on."

So I did.

Then I pushed open the curtain, stepped out, posed uncomfortably (head down; whole body slouched, curved inward; arms stiff with hands out helplessly and fingers splayed; left foot and toes curled under, dragging behind) as she regarded me. I wanted to die.

"Take it off. It looks horrible."

Off to a good start, as always.

"Try this [Biella Collezioni black wool pantsuit, crisp white Comme des Garçons blouse, same Clergerie boots]."

Again, I did.

"Better. But I don't love it."

Neither did I.

"Listen," I said. "I'm not sure these outfits are me. I mean, I'm not sure they're saying what I want to say. I think, in fact, they're saying too much. They make me feel overdressed, like I'm trying too hard. And the last thing I want her to think is that I spent hours and hours picking out what I'm going to wear."

"Even if you did."

"Right."

"So you want something simple, classic, chic. Something that looks like you just threw it on because you couldn't give a fuck."

"Exactly."

"Like, 'Go ahead. Steal my boyfriend.' "

"Fiancé."

"Whatever." She stared at me, then at the racks. "Here," she said, holding up an enormously oversized luxurious black sweater and shoving it through the curtain.

I grabbed it from her, slipped it over my head, fell in love with it immediately. I knew instantly that it was Adrienne-worthy.

"Let me see," she ordered, whipping open the curtain. She regarded me carefully. "I love it."

"Me too," I said, running my hands over the expanse of impossibly soft wool, and angling around toward the mirror. "What is it?"

"Eskandar. Cashmere."

"How much?"

"A lot."

"What's a lot?"

"Five hundred dollars."

"Oh." I stepped back, looked again, tried to talk myself out of it. Which was impossible: I had to have the sweater. And after a few seconds of creative justificatory mathematics (I'd saved money by not going to New York to shop; anything I'd have bought there combined with the airfare, taxis, lunch, and miscellaneous expenses would have been at least as much as the sweater; if I paid it off by fifty dollars a month, over, say, two years, I'd barely notice it), I'd even melted away the guilt.

"Okay, I'll take it," I said, still staring at myself in the mirror. "But does it make me look tall?"

"No."

I was flummoxed. "I want—I need—to look as tall as possible."

"Elise," she said heavily, with the tone of someone about to tell me the cold, hard truth. Which was the tone Fran always used. "You're not tall. You'll never be tall. Five-hundred-dollar Eskandar sweater or no five-hundred-dollar Eskandar sweater."

I felt the panic bubble up, then settle back down.

She put her arm around my neck; Bill Murray about to give Gilda Radner a noogie.

"So. Shorty," she said. "What's it gonna be? Do you want the sweater or not?"

I felt paralyzed.

"Think about it this way: You need the sweater. Every time you look at Adrienne and think how fabulous she is, you'll look down at this sweater and think how fabulous you are."

I nodded eagerly, hungry for this exact kind of existential self-actualizing wisdom—the kind I secretly longed for but never found in any of the books I worked on.

"You'll think how fabulous you are for having a friend as smart as me. A friend smart enough to find you a sweater as fabulous as this."

Despite the lack of deep meaning and philosophical resonance in her mini-speech, and the brilliantly soft hard sell she'd just done on me, disappointment quickly gave way to relief:

Five hundred dollars of (additional) credit card debt was nothing compared to the idea of spending the rest of my life alone.

10

Saturday arrived with unjust speed, and before I knew it, I was driving over to Gayle's house in Georgetown en route to the airport. She got into Donald's sleek black giant five-speed BMW 740, which I could barely handle without lurching and stalling—I feared my easy-to-maneuver stick-shift Jetta wouldn't have as much legroom for the Attenuated One—looking fantastic, having picked out a visually pleasing outfit today despite her usually odd and often misguided love of clothes with texture and color.

Wearing a black ribbed sweater set (texture), and a long wildly patterned sarong skirt (color), she slid into the front seat and shut the door, marveling, as she did, at the perfect *thunk!* sound it made ("Those Germans," she said admiringly, and with a near-perfect German accent, "certainly know how to design and build cars!" To which I added: "And crematoria") and kissed me—*peck, peck!* European-style—on both cheeks.

"Look!" she said excitedly, pointing to the black blazer she carried, unworn, in her lap. "Cast-off!"

She was referring, of course, to the term she used for anything—and everything—she salvaged from friends' for-charity piles. So passionate was she about anything free (coats, shoes, lunch, advice) that she once took every last second-rate cookbook a friend (the food critic of a big Maryland daily newspaper) was giving away. Prompting the critic-friend to speculate aloud to mutual friends that maybe Gayle had some sort of obsessive-compulsive collecting disorder.

She poked at me with her long slender fingers. "Don't you remember this jacket?"

I thought a minute, waiting for some memory to surface, but none came.

"Barneys warehouse sale," she said, twisting the collar so the telltale label was visible. "Four years ago. You gave it to me because you said you had too many jackets exactly like it."

Right. Those were the days. When I lived in New York and the perfect-weight perfectly cut black blazer could be found practically every five minutes. But I had far more important things to worry about at the moment.

"It must swim on you," I said. Gayle was, on a fat day, a size two, and I was, on my thinnest, a six.

"Yes, well," she said, regally, in the manner of someone who had fallen on hard times and had to suffer indignities such as these at great personal cost. "I've had to make do."

"There but for the grace of God, right?"

"And the kindness of strangers!"

She laughed, an impish monkey with all its teeth showing in a mad little grin. Forgetting myself for an instant, I laughed, too. But when I remembered, I stopped immediately.

"So," she said, her eyes wide, blinking wildly. "Are you nervous?"

Adrienne's flight was due to land in about thirty-six minutes. I was about to meet the woman who would unhinge me, who would cause me to almost destroy my life because I could not accept the fact that her body was, among other things, longer than mine.

I was about to spend an entire day pretending to be at peace with my physical inferiorities (deformities) and comparatively loser-like career status; at peace with the fact that she was moving to (encroaching on) our city; at peace with the fact that she and Donald were friends (inappropriately close); at peace with the fact that I had no idea what their friendship meant (too much) and where it would lead (to no good).

My life—my future happiness—everything—hung in the balance.

I was so nervous that I shut the car engine off in the middle of P Street as if I were parking.

"No," I lied, with ample sarcasm. "I'm not nervous." I looked out at the impossibly quaint street—gas-lanterned, tree-lined, brick-paved—and quickly came to my senses and moved the car.

"God, you're brave!" Gayle whispered.

I turned my head slowly to face her. "Are you crazy?"

She blinked wildly again. "What do you mean?"

"I mean, *Are you crazy?*"

More blinking.

"Of course I'm nervous!" I almost shouted. "Just when things were going so well, she has to come and ruin it all! I mean, why is this happening? Why is she doing this?"

For once, Gayle thought before she spoke: "Perhaps there is a *reason*." She drew the word out and it hung in the air, between us in the front seat, for several long silent seconds.

"A reason," I said. "You mean, cosmically."

"Karmically," she clarified. She'd been taken to India by her bohemian parents nearly every summer since she was a child and these distinctions were felt passionately.

"Whatever."

"Yes," she agreed, "whatever."

I checked my watch: T minus thirty-two. I pulled the car over to the side of the street and parked for real. "Go on," I said.

"What do you mean?"

"I mean: Go on. Elaborate. Tell me what the reason is."

"Well I don't know!" she said with mock outrage. "I was just trying to, you know, put a sort of spin on things."

I tightened my grip on the steering wheel. "Help me," I said. "Seriously. I'm dying, here. Tell me something that will make me feel better."

"Look. Listen," Gayle started. She sputtered. She stammered.

"There absolutely *is* a reason for all of this. One's fiancé's ex-fiancée doesn't simply drop from the sky one day, completely out of the blue, and enter, or reenter, their lives, five months before their wedding day. Do you follow?"

Now I was the one blinking. "Yes, I follow."

"This is a test."

I searched her face. "A test of what?"

She searched my face, too, as if she were making up her answer as she went along. "A test of your love for Donald, of course," she said. "And of his love for you. It is a test of trust."

Of course it was. I know that now. Though at the time, I couldn't see the bigger picture; couldn't understand the enormity of the situation and what passing—or failing—would really mean.

I released my grip on the wheel, slumped in the leather seat until it squeaked. "I hate tests," I said.

"Yes, well, look, who doesn't?"

I scanned the dashboard and peered outside. Soft lights were flickering on behind leaded glass windows in town houses; cars were starting to move; people were walking around with takeout coffee. "What I mean is, I'm terrible at tests. I almost always fail them." I paused, then tugged needily at Gayle's bony elbow. "What if I fail this one?"

"That's exactly my point. Don't you see?"

"See what?" I felt lost, completely at sea. I could, for one sad sorry instant, see Donald, our home, our impending life together, everything I'd come to adore and finally have, slipping away.

"You can't fail this test. You simply, absolutely cannot. Do you not follow?"

Her formal negative, usually reserved to flag matters of great importance. Duly alerted, I sat up, took note.

"And neither can Donald," she said, rather pointedly.

Even though I didn't really know what Gayle meant by this until much later, my stomach sank: destiny (Adrienne) waited; gloom and doom loomed; failure was certainly at hand. I turned the ignition, signaled, and lurched abruptly out into the sleepy, slow-moving, Saturday morning traffic.

11

It occurred to me as we snaked through Georgetown, down Rock Creek Parkway, then under the Kennedy Center, around the Lincoln Memorial and over the bridge toward National Airport, that I was better prepared than I'd given myself credit for.

I'd done my homework. I'd survived the French beauticians; survived Fran; survived the shock of signing the credit card receipt for the sweater she'd sold me. The session of physical attenuation I'd had with Cynthia that morning was only a metaphor for what I'd really needed to do: Attenuate myself emotionally. Spiritually.

After all the dread, the preparation, the anticipation, the anxiety, I wanted to get this show on the road: I wanted to meet Adrienne already.

And why not?

Having studied that one photograph of her for over a year now, I felt, oddly, as if I knew her intimately—staring, as I had, at every inch of her that was visible (eyebrows; ears, hands, cleavage; bust line; thighs); imagining every inch of her that wasn't (rear, calves, ankles, feet). I'd even heard her voice (deep, throaty, with that unmistakable Yale accent—equal parts refinement, entitlement, smarty-pantsism, with trace elements of Continental Europe, England, and New England) in conversation.

Women obsessed with women are just as scary as men obsessed with women.

Somewhere along the way, curiosity and obsession had outweighed insecurity, until suddenly, I felt (how stupid was I?) ready for Adrienne.

But when I caught that first glamorous, windblown, just-off-the-shuttle-from-Manhattan-where-I-live-and-you-don't (anymore) glimpse, all that changed.

We were on the ramp approaching US Airways Shuttle's pas-

senger pickup area when we saw Adrienne standing there, in profile, waiting.

"Oh, no," I said. "That's her."

"Are you sure?" Gayle asked.

"Yes I'm sure!" I snapped. Of course I was sure. I'd seen the
pictures. Which had lied. For she was, impossibly, much more gorgeous in real life than she was on film.

"God, she's fantastic!" Gayle said aloud, without meaning to, I
think.

I turned to her and gave her a look of such hatred and rage
that she retracted her statement immediately.

"No, you see what I meant was . . . *She's* not fantastic! Her *coat*
is fantastic!"

I knew I should never have let Gayle come along.

"You're supposed to be on my side, remember?" I said, then
swatted at her, but she flinched, so all I got in was an unsatisfying
light smack on her upper arm.

"Of course I'm on your side!" she said, and then, when I didn't
respond, she added in desperation: "Look, I'm sorry!" She was still
staring out the window when she said that—her nose practically
pressed up against the glass—so her apology naturally lost most, if
not all, of its intended effect. "But I simply must find out where
she got that coat!"

I swerved over to the curb, backed up a few yards to reverse
and delay our approach (lest Adrienne see us fighting and arguing
about her), then shoved the gear stick into neutral and pulled up
on the parking brake. Clearly, we needed a moment to correct a
problematic situation: Adrienne wasn't even in the car yet and
Gayle was all over her.

"If you ask her about that fucking coat, Gayle," I said, very,
very slowly, "I'll never speak to you again." I gave the threat time to
settle in, take root, before finishing it off. "Do you follow?"

"Yes," she said, nodding. "I follow."

"Good." I put my hands back on the steering wheel, grabbed it tightly, took a deep breath. Then I released the parking brake, put the car into first, and lurched a few feet up the curb until I was within spitting distance of Adrienne and her coat (deep olive green, faux pony skin, knee length).

Gayle was right.

The coat was fantastic.

God only knew what lay beneath it.

I inched forward along the ramp, managing, somehow, for once, by sheer divine intervention, to downshift the five-speed ultimate driving machine, pull it over to the curb directly in front of Adrienne, and bring it to a complete stop without stalling and with only minimal lurching. I wanted to weep, suddenly, with gratitude for the feats of German auto engineering which had made such a miracle possible.

But then, I wanted to weep, period.

For there before me, in all her absolute prettier-than-me, sexier-than-me, taller-than-me glory, she stood. Adrienne. Close up. Finally. After all this time.

The human mind, when experiencing a shocking event, processes it as best it can: the eyes close; the brain shuts down; memory splits, divides, breaks itself into shards. There is only so much trauma one can absorb in a single instant. Fragments are what you remember: bits, pieces, flashes illuminating indelible horrors, crime scene camera bulbs going off. But what you remember, you'll never forget. Never ever ever.

I remember all those images with complete clarity, if in slow motion: the unspeakable idiocy on my part (staring, slurring of words, eyes bugging out of my head at the first sight of that unforgettable push-up bra and what it was pushing up beneath the aforementioned fantastic coat); the supreme serenity on hers (unbridled sexuality).

This was going to be far far worse than I'd already thought, I realized suddenly. And with sickening dread.

And she knew it.

Her face, as I approached, seemed to glow with the knowledge that she was watching my worst nightmare unfold before her very eyes.

I looked down at my stupid five-hundred-dollar Eskandar sweater and marveled at my stupidity. I had underestimated my opponent. I had underdressed. I had done myself in.

I knew I should have gone to New York to shop!

I remember a barrage of quick, involuntary thoughts (wish-fulfillment fantasies) taking over then: I wished that Donald's 740 had a mind of its own and would spontaneously accelerate, jump the curb, and run Adrienne over; I wished Donald and I had never met; I wished that I was anywhere in the world but where I was at that exact moment. But there was no escape. Not now. It was too late.

Having spotted us, Adrienne flashed a big, confident I-love-myself-because-everyone-else-does smile, which was almost as blinding as the mid-morning sun. I smiled (or tried desperately to, anyway) back, feverishly feeling up the door in search of the handle.

"Stay here!" I ordered Gayle, as I started to climb out of the car, but she had already leapt out on her side. We both approached the curb awkwardly, at the exact same time, and Adrienne looked at both of us, confused for a split second, it seemed, about who was who.

"You . . . must . . . be . . . Elise," she said eventually, extending her slender leather-gloved hand to me. "I'm Adrienne."

Yes, she certainly was.

It took me a few seconds to get over the shock of actually seeing her; almost immediately I found I couldn't quite make direct eye contact. It was like staring into the sun, or finally being next to a celebrity after waiting years to meet them. I glanced at her surreptiously, trying to take in as many details as I could as quickly as I could.

But there was her hand, outstretched.

I gave her my hand, too, and we shook. And as we did, I saw her eyes go directly to my other hand and the engagement ring on it. Of course, I didn't blame her: it was a beautiful ring; Donald did, after all, have very good taste. She registered it, said nothing, and I retracted my hand.

And we were off and running!

"Hi," I said.

"Hi," she said back.

I paused uncomfortably, then turned toward Gayle to introduce her. And when I did I noticed her mouth hanging open. I jabbed my elbow into Gayle's upper arm and ribs to snap her out of it, and she winced audibly. I ignored her.

"And this is my best friend, Gayle." I said, almost choking on the words—not just because this alleged best friend of mine was entranced by my nemesis, but because I was in my mid-thirties and still using the term "best friend."

"Hi!" said Gayle.

"Hi!" said Adrienne.

"Hi!" I said again.

Hi!

Hi!

Hi!

We all paused, silent for a split second, which felt like an hour in that wrinkle of time. Gayle licked her lips. I knew what was coming, but there was no stopping her.

"Look," she said, "I simply must know where you got that coat. It's fantastic!"

"I know!" Adrienne gushed back, running her hands down the lapel, the buttons, and both pockets. "Isn't it?"

And she was modest, too.

"I got it at Bergdorf's."

Gayle blinked. "This year?"

Adrienne hesitated, seemingly confused. "Yes."

Of course she'd bought it this year. Not everyone wore other people's four-year-old cast-offs.

Desperate to end the insufferable love fest going on in front of me, I interrupted with a barrage of banal questions for Adrienne even though I couldn't have cared less: *How was your flight? Were you waiting here long? Do you have any bags?*

"The flight was great," she said, flipping her thick straight shiny black hair from her mouth, then pulling away one single pesky strand which had become glued to her lip gloss. "It was actually a little bumpy even though it's completely clear up there. But I love to fly, so, it was fine."

No Jewish Gloom and Doom here. Adrienne, it seemed, had that adventurous, fearless, mountain-climbing spirit; she didn't see death and dying around every aisle and window seat, as I did.

"How ironic is that! Elise hates to fly!" Gayle chimed in, with blissful ignorance. "Once, we flew to Los Angeles together for a wedding, and she was grabbing my arm so tightly she left fingerprint and nail marks on the skin!" She pushed back the sleeve of her textured cardigan sweater to reveal her delicately sinewy arm and wrist, then dug the fingers of her other hand into the flesh there to simulate the high-altitude scene she'd just described.

"Yes, well," I retorted sorely, and as if it mattered or would help my case, "Donald hates to fly, too."

"That's *right*," Adrienne said, as if remembering some far-off memory. "He did."

"Does," I corrected.

Another pause, another awkward silence. I was finding it difficult to breathe.

"Well," I said with aggressive cheerfulness, motioning to the car with my hand. "Shall we?"

Adrienne and Gayle were all over each other again while I put Adrienne's (Louis Vuitton) garment bag into the trunk—Gayle touching the coat while Adrienne unbuttoned it to show off the fuschia satin lining inside. And when she unbuttoned it, I watched in horror as that quick simple movement revealed the magnitude of her bust line: the aforementioned push-up bra pushing her breasts up and into the deeply scoop-necked white T-shirt that barely grazed the belt loops of her skin-tight Diesel jeans.

I lost my breath; felt faint: hyperventilation, then flat-lining, seemed imminent. I tried to concentrate on breathing deeply, until I realized Gayle and Adrienne were both waiting to get let into the locked car. I hit the disarm button on my key chain, walked around to the passenger side of the car (Adrienne's coat was closed again, thank God, so my oxygen intake increased slightly) and opened the front door. But they were already climbing into the back seat together, still talking about that infernal coat, so I slammed the door and walked back to my side.

I got in and slumped behind the wheel. I felt like a limousine driver, staring at them like that in the rearview mirror.

"This is just like *Driving Miss Daisy*," I said to no one in particular.

They both giggled.

I wished they were dead.

"Listen!" Gayle said, leaning over the front seat so I could hear her. "I was just telling Adrienne about Fran's store. And she said she'd love to get in a shop!"

Get in a shop?

"Would she now," I said, feigning delight.

"Yes, she would!" Adrienne said, then she and Gayle giggled again.

The idea quickly started to grow on me. I realized that I, too, wanted her to get in a shop:

Out of loyalty to me (I had, after all, just dropped five hundred dollars on a sweater I now hated), Fran would eat her for breakfast.

First things first, though.

Adrienne was staying overnight, so we dropped her bag off with the concierge of the tony but tainted Jefferson Hotel (Dick Morris, I was happy to recall, had besmirched himself publicly there with a woman of ill repute) and waited while she checked in (duly impressed by her bust line—it seemed her coat had somehow managed to fall open again—the little man at the front desk instantly upgraded her deluxe room to a suite, which Adrienne barely acknowledged. This type of thing must happen to her all the time, I thought with disgust).

Back in the car, we drove up Connecticut Avenue to Politics and Prose bookstore, and sat down in their coffeehouse amongst the throngs of bearded, Birkenstock-footed, NPR T-shirt-wearing, weekend-morning patrons. The three of us stuck out like sore thumbs. After a moment of silent discomfort and acclimation, I pointed toward the espresso bar, where we selected from a vast array of clever drink concoctions noted on the chalkboard ("Just for the Chai of it"; "Changes in Latte-tude"; "La Ca-Puccini") and commenced to plan the day.

As the one at the table who was, by far, the least mentally stable and the one who had the most to lose, I took the lead. Out of my bag came a notebook, pen, pencil, legal pad, Fodor's guide to Washington, two back issues of *Washingtonian* magazine, the classified section of that morning's *Washington Post*, and an elastic band (I have no idea what the elastic band was for, but I was somehow comforted by its presence).

"Elise is an absolute *genius* at planning things," Gayle said to Adrienne. "She's so organized, and clear-thinking, and—"

"Neurotic," I said. I tried to smile, give myself a lift ("Those who can laugh at themselves don't get laughed at," or however the saying went). "Go ahead," I nodded at Gayle. "You can say it."

"Well, yes, then," Gayle said, a little too quickly for my liking. "Certainly neurotic."

Adrienne raised an eyebrow, taking note.

"You're in the best of hands, really, I promise you," Gayle continued. "She leaves nothing to chance and thinks of everything. You'll find a terrific apartment, buy some fabulous clothes, and have a wonderful tour of the city all before you leave tomorrow!"

I tried to kick Gayle under the table. She was, as usual, going way too far. She was starting to sound shifty, desperate, as if she were trying to sell ice to an Eskimo.

An Eskimo in an olive green faux-pony-skin coat who shopped at Bergdorf's.

"That's quite a buildup," Adrienne said, with mock enthusiasm and unmistakable condescension, for Gayle had unwittingly made my "talents" sound silly and inane. Organized women (like me) were immediately dismissed by disorganized women (like Adrienne): it was an issue of power. Organized women were not leaders, creative thinkers, big-picture types. They were "support staff," obsessed with details, mired in the micro—secretaries; assistants; household help; wives.

Speaking of which: "Donald's very lucky to be marrying someone as capable as you."

I looked down at the ridiculous array of day-planning materials spread out in front of me on the table and wished I could have made myself disappear. But I couldn't. As Dr. Frond used to say, I had to learn to "sit with" my discomfort, endure it, transcend it.

"*Anyway* . . . " I said, wanting desperately to bite Adrienne and to pretend the whole morning thus far hadn't happened. "I've made a lunch reservation for us at the Hay-Adams dining room at one o'clock. It's one of the prettiest rooms here, with a lovely view of Lafayette Park," I said, like I cared, and like I knew for certain that it was Lafayette Park and not Lafayette Square I was talking about (it took me the whole day to remember that it was the square, actually). "So until then, we can run around and look at as many apartments as we need to." I pulled out the *Washington Post* classifieds and slid them toward her. "I've made notes and circled some possibilities, so the search will be somewhat targeted."

"That is so kind of you, Elise. But actually, the search will be very targeted," Adrienne said. "A friend of my father's at Air and Space here has found me an apartment in the Kennedy-Warren."

I nodded bitterly. Only the best for Adrienne.

The Kennedy-Warren was the most historically significant rental building in the city. It was also known to be one of the most sophisticated, filled as it was with lots of ex–New Yorkers who were journalists, novelists, television pundits — transplants to Washington whose jobs paid better than freelance copyediting. I would've killed for an apartment there when I first moved. Set back from the street with its stately façade and grounds, the building was located right in the heart of our beloved Cleveland Park. She was like a heat-seeking missile, this woman, programmed to destroy my life with breathtaking precision.

"They're holding it for me. So . . . " she continued, voice singsong, eyebrows raised to imply it was all going to be a piece of cake, "assuming I like it, and I'm sure I will, I'll give them a check, fill out the paperwork, take a few measurements, and then we'll be free until dinner."

"Dinner?" Gayle said, looking lost.

Donald's grilled dinner. To which I hadn't invited her.

"Yes, dinner," Adrienne said, "at Elise and Donald's. Donald's going to cook."

"Donald's going to *grill*," I clarified.

There was a difference. A big difference. Cooking was decidedly feminine, grilling was not; cooking required a degree of skill and finesse, grilling did not; cooking was relatively safe with minimal risk to flesh and limb, grilling was (hopefully) not.

"Sounds lovely," Gayle said, sighing: Cinderella kept back from the ball.

"Aren't you coming?" Adrienne asked, knowing full well she wasn't. It was just supposed to be the four of us: Adrienne, me, Donald, and Terrance, a friend (single, male, attractive enough) of Donald's (my idea) from work. Not four plus a one-woman cheering section for Adrienne.

"Well . . . no . . . I . . ."

"Oh, *please!*" she said with excessive emotion. "You *must* come!"

It was official: the evening—my life—my future—was completely out of control.

"So you'll be there?" Adrienne asked, waiting, with bated breath, for Gayle's immediate verbal RSVP. "That's okay, isn't it, Elise?"

"Yes of course!" Gayle said, even before I had a chance to answer. "I'd love to!"

They hugged, Adrienne claiming Gayle as her ally, Gayle an innocent, unwitting, well-intentioned pawn in this unhappy marriage, a child who just wanted to be loved.

"To the Kennedy-Warren then," said Gayle, as we approached the car and they slid into the back seat. And I obliged.

The apartment—two bedrooms, two full baths, a huge living room, dining room, kitchen, and sun-room on the seventh floor—all (save for the bathrooms) with spectacular views of Rock Creek Park and the National Zoo—was, as expected, perfect. Adrienne marched from room to room, inspecting closets, kitchen cabinets, assessing spatial relationships. The possibilities, like her bust line (her coat was not just open, now, but off), were endless. Finding everything to her liking—or almost everything, I should say: she wasn't crazy about the medicine cabinet in the second bathroom, or about the original metal latches on the kitchen cabinets which were, as yet, unpolished (the princess and the pea, was she)—we returned to the lobby (famous for its stunning art deco detail, which she knew all about, having majored in art history at Yale, she somehow found it necessary to inform the building manager who was escorting us) to complete the rental transaction.

Adrienne disappeared into the office to sign the lease and discuss moving details; Gayle and I sank into a plush pink sofa by the window and waited.

"So! What do you think?" Gayle said, full of nervous energy beside me. We hadn't had a minute alone since Adrienne had stepped off the plane, and she was desperate to compare notes.

"I think . . . " I started slowly, tauntingly, mysteriously, "that you . . . "

She nodded expectantly.

". . . are . . . "

More nodding, licking of the lips, wringing of the hands.

". . . in big trouble."

She laughed, poked my arm. Surely I was pulling her leg.

"Oh, I'm quite serious. I assure you."

She looked shocked. "But why?"

"Why? You're all over her! It's like you're in love with her! This *was* supposed to be the easy part of the day—this Donald-less part. But with all your mooning and swooning and incessant fawning, tonight will be a breeze." I shook my head in disgust. "That's right! Dinner tonight, in *my* home, with *my* fiancé who used to be *her* fiancé—the dinner which you were invited to *not* by me, the official hostess, but by her"—and I motioned heatedly toward my bust here—"the one with the *most*-ess—now looks like a fucking piece of cake, thanks to you!"

"God, I'm sorry! I had no idea I was doing anything wrong! It's just that, well, you see, I'm nervous, very nervous—for you—and so it's come out this way."

"Well, stop it," I said.

"Yes."

"I mean it. Please. Cut it out."

"Yes."

I stared at her, making sure she understood what was at stake: her health and well-being; our friendship; my future with Donald.

"Yes," she said, deeply, though fleetingly I knew, apologetic. "I—"

"You better follow."

Adrienne returned then, slipping an envelope into her (Hermes Birkin) bag (I was dying to know where she got her money; I strongly suspected a trust fund). We three were silent again, momentarily; at a complete loss for words and for what should come next. It was only noon, and we were ahead of schedule. So out of complete desperation I suggested we head back downtown for lunch.

"I'm sure the Hay-Adams will seat us early," I said, walking toward the car.

Adrienne agreed. "I'm sure they will," she said, and just then her coat fell open.

I looked at her again. I was sure they would seat us on the moon.

13

"This is *lovely*, Elise," Adrienne said as we walked through the lobby and into the dining room of the Hay-Adams Hotel. "Just *lovely*. What a perfect spot for lunch."

Translation:

Dowdy. Boring. Historical. Dull.

"I'm glad you like it," I said. I looked around the pretty yellow room, filled with well-to-do mostly middle-aged tourists, businessmen, and ladies-who-lunch, and wanted to slap myself. What had I been thinking?

"A girl's lunch! Yes, it's absolutely perfect!" Gayle chimed in.

"Well, it's not the Plaza, or the Mark, or the St. Regis, or the Royalton—" I could have gone on and on and on, rattling off hotels like an idiot, trying to impress her with my knowledge of Manhattan, but all it did was make me look desperate. I reached for my water glass and took a long, slow sip to cleanse my palate and ruminate. Just invoking the names of all those great hotels made me sad, and long for New York.

When I looked up again, Adrienne's eyes seemed to have softened. Head tilted, she regarded me and smiled. She knew, implicitly, that I was nervous and unbearably uncomfortable in her presence, and while one part of her positively thrived on that perfect morsel of knowledge and was empowered by it, another part pitied me for it. I didn't know which part was worse.

"And I really appreciate your taking so much time for me. I know how busy you must be planning your wedding." She glanced at the menu, set it aside, then looked around the dining room, which she seemed to find decidedly uninteresting. "I keep meaning to ask you—where's it going to be?"

"Dumbarton House. In Georgetown."

Her face lit up. "How lovely. The gardens are exquisite."

"Spectacular," Gayle, the new Queen of Hyperbole, chimed in.

"Kay"—Adrienne regarded us both solemnly, to clarify and to respectfully acknowledge her subject's recent death—"Kay *Graham*, of the *Washington Post*, used to take me there when I was little and we'd come to visit. She lived right around the corner. My father and Ben"—she stopped again to clarify—"Ben *Bradlee*—went to college together." She shrugged as if to communicate humility. "Actually, he's my godfather."

I blinked madly; sat dumbfounded; tried desperately, and failed miserably, to think of a comeback.

"Gayle here knows Frank Perdue," I offered sarcastically. "In fact, she wrote a whole book about him." I elbowed her gently and smiled, trying to encourage her to participate in the shameless name-dropping that Adrienne had started. But Gayle was too starstruck to pick up on my less-than-subtle hints.

"God, I've always thought Ben Bradlee was one of the sexiest men in the whole world."

Adrienne's eyes widened. "Do you know him?"

"Well, I met him several times, when I used to contribute pieces to the *Post*."

"*Really*! What kinds of pieces did you do?"

"Food pieces, mostly. I love food, you see."

Boy, did she ever.

"So does he!" Adrienne marveled.

"Yes! And it seemed every time I was there to turn my copy in—this was before computers and faxes and email, remember, so one had to deliver things by hand—he would ask me about what I'd written: the dish, the preparation, the ingredients, special techniques and equipment. Asian food was just coming into vogue then and everyone was stir-frying like crazy!"

Knowing nobody from the *Post* and hating to cook, I sat quietly, glanced around the restaurant until the conversation swung around to a topic I might be able to participate in.

"So Donald tells me you're in graduate school," Adrienne said, turning back to me. "For . . . ?"

"A master's."

"In . . . ?"

"Education."

"At . . . ?"

"Georgetown."

"Right," she said, as if vaguely remembering the specifics of my humble aspirations. "You hope to teach someday?"

I nodded, then winced. The way she said "teach" sounded as if she was articulating my hope to someday be able to walk and talk at the same time.

She looked incredulous. "I can't *imagine* being back in school. Not at this age."

"And what age is that?" I couldn't help myself.

"Twenty-nine."

Twenty-nine.

She turned to Gayle again, hoping to change the subject to something more interesting. "So what do *you* do?"

"I'm a reporter."

"Really." She sounded duly impressed. "For what publication?"

"*Congressional Quarterly.*"

"Oh! *CQ!*"

"Yes! *CQ!*" Gayle looked delighted. Finally, someone who was familiar enough with the magazine to call it by its insiderly abbreviation.

I drummed my fingers on the table, tempted to add that I liked to refer to it by my own personal favorite nickname—*The House Organ*—but I didn't. After several minutes of listening to Adrienne and Gayle gab away about whom they knew in common at the magazine and how interesting it must be to cover politics, though, I ran out of patience.

"Yes, Gayle's been covering the flag debate since the beginning. In fact, I think she broke the story."

"What flag debate?" Adrienne asked.

Gayle blushed.

"Well, there's two issues, actually, right, Gayle?"

"Right."

"There's the Pledge of Allegiance issue, and then there's the flag desecration constitutional amendment that's still pending. Both, of course, very very big in this town."

Adrienne started to glaze over. "*Really*," she said, trying to sound interested enough to be polite but not so interested as to keep this line of conversation going. "Stories like this never seem to make the *Times*."

"Sometimes they don't even make the *Post*," I added under my breath.

"*Anyway*, back to the wedding," Adrienne said, clearly relieved to have found a segue. "Will it be a day or evening affair?"

"A Saturday evening."

"So, it'll be formal."

"Actually, it'll be semi-formal"

I had no idea what I was talking about.

"Oh." She leaned back in her chair and squeezed the life out of a wedge of lemon into her glass of iced tea. "I never know what that means, *semi*-formal, on an invitation. Does one wear a cocktail dress? A suit? A long dress?"

Like it mattered. She wasn't coming.

"I often wish people were more definitive," she continued. "*Absolutely formal*. Or *absolutely informal*." She shook her head, sipped from her glass. "But that's just me, I suppose."

Gayle nodded. "Yes, I agree *completely*. I much prefer things to be definitive."

I glared at her. "What things?"

"Well, *things*, you know. Dinners, parties, weddings, other events and such."

"Since when are you a stickler for being definitive? You're the most vague, inexact, confused person I've ever known."

Gayle looked wounded. Those were the things I always said I most loved about her.

"I was kidding," I said, and she was immediately resuscitated. But the damage had already been done as far as Adrienne was concerned. She could tell I was lashing out because I was nervous. Either that or she'd decided I was simply a bitch.

"So back to the wedding." Clearly, Adrienne did not want to let the subject go. "Will you be having a religious ceremony?"

"We're not sure yet. It's complicated, given the fact that we're of different faiths."

"Not to mention the fact that Dumbarton House is run by the Daughters of the American Revolution. I can't imagine they're that comfortable with the idea of a *chuppah*."

"I know," I said.

"Me, too." She smiled knowingly. "I'm half-Jewish."

"Really? Which half?" Like it mattered.

"My father is a German Jew; my mother is French."

"French-French, or Canadian-French?" I couldn't help myself.

"French-French," she replied. "She is from France."

Catherine Deneuve; not Celine Dion.

Missing the mean-spirited subtleties, as always, Gayle looked perplexed. "Of *course* Adrienne is French-French! Very few Canadians would have the *courage* to select—let alone carry off—a coat like hers. I mean, this is an incredibly sophisticated coat."

Again with the coat. And the hyperbole.

"Now, the French have some wonderful wedding traditions, don't they?" Gayle continued.

"Actually, we do. There's the *coupe de mariage*, a special cup the bride and groom drink from when they make their special toast. Then, of course, there's the fact that, like French meals, French weddings are incredibly long and drawn out. And then there's *poster les bans*."

"What's that?" Gayle asked on cue.

"A few weeks before a French couple is married, they put up a notice at the city hall to make sure there are no objections."

I imagined Adrienne putting up such a sign and a stampede of men crashing into the bulletin board, ripping and tearing at the sign and voicing their desperate objections in the hope that she'd change her mind and marry one of them. Then I imagined putting a sign up myself and Adrienne begging Donald to ditch me and marry her.

The waiter approached, refilled our water glasses; took our lunch orders. Which were all the same: Cobb salads. None of us, it seemed, wanted to have a protruding paunch later in the afternoon while trying on clothes at Embellish.

"And what's the date?" She looked at Gayle, her new best friend, and rolled her eyes. "I couldn't get anything out of Donald the other day when we spoke. It was like he was guarding state secrets."

"April," I said. "April fifteenth."

Adrienne stared at me, then stirred her iced tea. "April fifteenth," she said. "How funny."

"Why is it funny?"

"Well, it's funny because, as I'm sure you know, that was our wedding date, Donald's and mine. What was to be our wedding date, I mean," she said, "before we broke it off."

Shocked to the core, my heart pounded, my hands shook. To calm myself, I busily wiped nonexistent crumbs off the pristine heavy white linen tablecloth. Which reminded me suddenly that I hadn't yet picked our table linens.

The table linens for the wedding.

Our wedding.

Donald's and mine.

The one that was to be held on April fifteenth of this coming year with me and him, not April fifteenth of seven years ago with him and Adrienne.

My mind raced, searched for a response. Miraculously, one (a big huge ballooning lie) appeared.

"Of course I know. But for various reasons, the fifteenth was the best date for everyone involved." I sat back, satisfied with the breadth and scope of my grand falsehood and marveling at the calming effect the act of lying was having on my nervous system. Then I lowered my voice to a whisper, as if about to impart a secret of the utmost sanctity: "Plus, he felt very strongly about that date for us. *Very* strongly."

Very strongly *against* it.

As Adrienne and Gayle chatted away and their voices became a blur, I thought back to when we had picked that date, and I tried to remember exactly what he'd said when, for whatever reasons at the time (the convenience of our many New York–based out-of-town guests; the availability of venues and caterers and non-religious personnel; the mere sound of it), I had announced with absolute conviction:

"April fifteenth."

"Oh God, no! Not the fifteenth!" he had said. It was all coming back to me now.

"What's wrong with the fifteenth?"

He blanched, looked away, played with his hands. "Nothing. It's just . . . well . . . it's nothing. Never mind."

"No," I insisted. "What's wrong with it?"

"It just has bad associations for me, that's all."

"Bad childhood associations?" I asked. I was thinking specifically of all that nonsense with his mother's forcing him to cook and the alleged ensuing trauma. "Does this have something to do with your fear of being feminized?"

"No. No. No." He shook his head, waved his hands. *If only!* he seemed to be pantomiming.

"Then what? Basketball? Football?" He seemed, in retrospect, to be racking his brain for a suitable explanation, for something other than the truth. But at the time, I thought it was just one of his minor breakdowns. "It's just . . . well . . . " and then he blurted: "Well, it's *tax* day."

"Tax day? So what?"

He shrugged, unable to speak.

"We'll file our returns by then—before then, even, if you want," I'd said, trying hard to sound reassuring but suspecting, correctly I saw now, that he was already beyond help.

"Yes, well, I'm sure we will. But it's just that, you know, tax day doesn't seem to be the appropriate day to have our wedding. Our anniversary, then, would always be on April fifteenth, and an otherwise memorable and romantic occasion would always be associated with deductions, and forms, and calculations, and memories of Ad—"

"Addition? Subtraction? Math?" Was there another latent phobia I knew nothing about? Yet another layer to my beloved, troubled Sybil?

"Yes, *math*." He stopped, sighed, spent with (false) confession, great relief. "I'd just rather not have our happiest, most important moment together immortalized and minimized by stress."

"You certainly have a point," I said, stretching the truth just a little bit (he had *a* point; not, in my mind, a terribly important one). If I'd only known. "But April fifteenth is the only date that works"—and here I pulled out all the charts and spreadsheets and file folders and legal pads and schedules and date books and wedding planners, the tools of my trade—"until August."

He glanced at the table, then closed his eyes, and nodded. "Whatever."

And that was when, like a fool, I promised we'd file early every year, so that by the time our anniversary rolled around, we'd be opening our refunds.

By the time our salads finally came, brimming with bits and shreds and crumbs and chunks of blue cheese, chicken, avocado, bacon, and tomato, I had completely lost my appetite. The sight of my food sickened me, so full of anxiety was I now about the certain fiasco our wedding day—not to mention marriage—would be; I stared down at the plate but didn't touch it. Adrienne stared at her plate, too, but didn't touch hers either. The only one of us who ate—voraciously, gleefully—was Gayle.

"I'm *famished!*" she announced between bites, her mouth full of food and practically splitting at the seams.

Of course she was. Anyone would be after all that ass-kissing.

Seeing Gayle eat with such wild abandon for the first time, Adrienne must have feared she was truly and seriously undernourished. Pushing her plate discreetly across the table and touching Gayle on the arm, she said: "Here. You eat mine. I had a late breakfast."

(One strawberry, two grapes, I imagined.)

Gayle licked her lips, then devoured much of Adrienne's plate, too.

And after a round of coffee and the check, which Adrienne insisted on picking up, we left the dining room and headed up to Fran's store.

14

Certain of the blatant rudeness, inescapable torture, and deeply scarring psychological damage Fran would surely inflict on Adrienne, I opened the moon roof and gunned the engine up Connecticut Avenue, through Dupont Circle, on past the zoo and over to Chevy Chase.

Nestled between Cartier and Versace, just blocks away from Neiman's, Saks, and Tiffany, lay my spider's web. We parked in the lot across the street and I led the way with a spring in my step. Adrienne would be toast.

It was the least suicidal I'd been all day.

But, despite Fran's I'll-take-care-of-this-one wink when we first entered the store (I'd called her on my cell phone, from the ladies' room of the Hay-Adams, to give her a heads-up that we were coming), she, too, fell under the spell of Adrienne.

First, there was the Attenuated One's figure, which looked "fabulous" (Fran's word, not mine) in anything—and everything—pushed through the purple velvet curtain for her to try on (no gigantic, oversized, body-hiding Eskandar sweaters this time). Then, there were her cash reserves and her willingness to spend them: she bought two sweaters (clingy), a pair of pants (tight), and one floor-length evening dress (positively painted on) in just under forty-two minutes, and I doubted she'd be on the twenty-four-month payment plan like I was. To top it all off, there was her impressive and, of course, firsthand knowledge of avant-garde designers and their wares: Dries Van Noten's Belgian mother and her mother had met in postwar France and had stayed in touch over the years, Dries sending Adrienne, his young distant-cousin American muse, boxes of clothes gratis from his Antwerp studio.

Fran was practically drooling. Racing back and forth from the racks to the dressing room (the only time I'd seen her move that fast was when she had to pee) and fetching bottled water (for Adrienne) and hot tea and cookies (for Gayle) from the back room (I'd never even known there was a back room, let alone that it contained beverages and provisions), the only thing she bothered to say to me was this:

"She's a fucking knockout."

Translation?

That Donald of yours must really be an asswipe to have let her *get away.*

And I can't say I disagreed. Maybe he was a loser to have ended up with me.

Silent, sullen, and certain, now, that the dinner which lay ahead would only serve to showcase Adrienne's excessive attributes even more than her excessive attributes had already been showcased (simply by her being awake and standing), I decided to be proactive and put an end to this infernal afternoon.

First, I dropped Adrienne off at the Jefferson Hotel, politely declining her invitation to join her for afternoon tea off the lobby. Three doormen, two porters, and one parking valet fell all over each other as they lunged for the car door in order to be the one to escort her into the lobby (the parking valet won, since he was the only manservant over five and a half feet tall).

Typical.

Next, I dropped Gayle off in Georgetown. After having endured my silence all the way from the hotel to her house, she crawled out of the back seat and waved at me through the glass, obsequiously, apologetically, while mouthing the words "look" and "listen" in an attempt to explain her behavior, but I kept my window rolled up. What was there to explain? My best friend had sealed my fate in this unspoken competition: Adrienne had won the day, and would not take her victory lightly vis-à-vis tonight's dinner with Donald. God only knew what lay in store for me!

Pushier push-up bras? Glossier lip gloss? I catalogued the unthinkable as I lurched off down P Street.

Finally, I stopped at a liquor store on the way home far up on Connecticut Avenue. I stood there for a few long minutes, caressing a giant bottle of Jack Daniel's and gazing lustfully at a wall of cigarettes. But I walked out empty-handed.

There wasn't enough bourbon or tobacco in the world.

I returned home a few minutes past four (dinner would not be served until eight) and when I did I found Donald in the kitchen, surrounded by jars and books and containers of every shape and sort. The counters were a disaster (had he deliberately coated them in butter, or had it simply been an accident?); the refrigerator a mess (he'd obviously removed everything at least once, then put it all back in search of something as easy to find as mustard); the sink an inch deep in garlic peels, onion skins, scallion and chive and shallot butts. It was Williams-Sonoma on acid. I looked at the culinary tableau, the resplendent mess, with a heavy, heavy heart: our life, as I'd known it, would soon be over.

The Age of Adrienne was now upon us.

"You're home!" Donald effused, throwing three heavy-handled forged knives into the sink (they were like golf clubs, he always said—he never knew which one to use), wiped his hands on his apron (frilly, flowered, and flagrantly feminine—it had been a gift, as a joke, from me), and flew across the kitchen toward me. He grabbed me by the hand, encircled my waist (such as it was, my obesity hidden under all that expensive Eskandar cashmere) with his arms, and nuzzled my ear. I could tell he felt a dance coming on.

I hung on for dear life.

"I missed you," he said, kissing me on the forehead. "As soon as you left this morning, I realized what an incredibly stupid thing I'd done—letting you spend the entire day with Adrienne."

I bet he regretted it. Had he gotten nervous, had second thoughts, about the idea of Adrienne and me getting to know each other? At the prospect (however far-fetched) of Adrienne and me becoming friends? Was he afraid we'd talk about him? Compare notes? Share secrets?

"And I never should have invited her for dinner. I mean, now we have her, and Terrance—"

"And Gayle." I added.

"And Gayle?" He looked worriedly at the vast amounts of food marinating and ready to grill as if there somehow wouldn't be enough (he had seen Gayle pack it away many times, so he actually could have been right).

"Adrienne invited her." I let the sentence hang there in the air, like a little noose, ready to tighten around her attenuated Audrey Hepburn–like neck: Donald was nothing if not a stickler for the strict maintenance of social etiquette.

He rolled his eyes. "So now we have her and Terrance and Gayle coming over and—God," he whispered sadly, "I *hate* people. The only person in the world I like is you, and well, you live here. But I guess—well—it's our first dinner party."

And maybe our last.

"Look! I'm marinating!" he announced, with heartbreaking pride and excitement, so I went over to pay my respects to the pan of swordfish steaks swimming in olive oil and a white creamy horseradish sauce. I stared into it, as if those thick slabs of raw fish could tell me my fate. But they gave up nothing. Except for a fairly pungent odor. A wave of mild nausea made a beeline for my gullet.

"Smells—"

"Good?" Donald looked at me expectantly.

"No. Fishy."

"Fishy?"

I nodded.

"Oh. Bad-fishy or good-fishy?"

"There is no good-fishy."

"There isn't?"

"No."

He nodded. Of course there wasn't. He stared into the pan, now, too, and sniffed loudly. "Are you sure it smells fishy?"

As of today, I was sure of nothing.

"Because I don't smell anything."

Of course he didn't smell anything. He was a guy. And guys could never distinguish between edible food and rotten food; good women and highly manipulative, troublemaking women.

"Maybe it's the horseradish."

No.

He stuck his nose into the pan again and sniffed. "Really, Elise, it smells fine to me. I just bought it this morning from Fresh Fields and they said it was caught yesterday. But, what, you think I should just dump it?"

"Maybe it's just my imagination."

Maybe it was. Weren't olfactory hallucinations the first sign of severe mental disturbance?

He sniffed again, shifted his weight, prepared to take a stance. "I think it is your imagination. The fish is fine. I'm going to serve it."

I shrugged. "Okay."

I couldn't have cared less. Let them all eat rotten fish and get salmonella poisoning. Let them all eat perfectly good fish and fall in love with each other. I myself was too obese to ever eat again anyway.

Now that his main dinner entrée was salvaged, he untied his apron, lifted it over his head, flung it toward the table (it hit the side, slid down the leg, and settled into a poufy pile on the floor), and finally addressed the pink elephant in the room: my day with Adrienne.

"So?" he asked.

"So, what?"

"How was it?"

"How was what?"

"*It.*"

"It?" I was going to make him work for this.

"Adrienne."

I stared blankly, fell mute. There were no words to describe her, really.

"Great."

"*Really.*" He sounded surprised, and fascinated; then looked nervous. Very nervous. There was a long silence—long for Donald and me. Finally, with his eyes lowered, he asked: "Did you talk about me?"

"No." Well, I wasn't going to bring up the subject of the wedding date. Not yet.

"Why was it so great then?"

"It wasn't great. I was being sarcastic."

Donald blinked. *Uh*-oh.

"In the pantheon of bad experiences I've had during the course of my lifetime—and, as you know, I've had many many experiences I'd classify as bad—I'd have to say it was, without comparison, the worst day I've ever had."

Donald nodded vigorously, completely rapt. "Why?"

"Why? Well," I said slowly, "for starters, she's gorgeous."

"So are you!"

"Ha!" I laughed. What a lame attempt to defuse me!

"You are! Why do you think I'm marrying you?"

"Shut up."

"I mean, of course, that's not the only reason I'm marrying you. . . ."

"Please shut up."

"I'm serious," he insisted.

"We're not talking about me now. We're talking about her."

He flapped his hands in frustration. "I wouldn't say she's gorgeous—"

"Oh really? What would you say?"

He scratched his head, suddenly speechless.

"How about 'stacked'?" I offered. I had no idea where that word, a relic of *Playboy* magazine–speak, had come from, but I embraced it, then raged past it. "I mean, she was dressed like a— like a"—I searched for the words and while I did I could see Donald bracing himself, as if he were watching the fuse of a piece of dynamite burn dangerously close to the end on a Road Runner and Wile E. Coyote cartoon—"a fucking teenager!"

He paused, attempting to envision that.

"Yes," I poked him in the stomach. "Like a teenager! A slutty teenager! A slutty teenager trying to seduce her French teacher! Or her lacrosse coach! Or her field hockey coach! Or whatever she played in high school, or boarding school. I'm sure she was a real ace."

"Was she *really* dressed like a slutty teenager?"

He sounded a little too interested for my liking.

"I mean, she never looked like that when I knew her," he said.

"Sure."

"No, I swear!"

"What, no push-up bras?"

He shook his head.

"No deeply scoop-necked T-shirts?"

He shook his head again.

"No skintight ass-hugging pants?"

"No! She used to wear jeans and overalls! Big sweaters and turtlenecks! She was very—plain."

I thought of the section of the Victoria's Secret catalogue where the models wear cotton bras and panties and thongs, instead of silk and satin and lace ones. Plain. My ass.

"Oh, come on, Elise. You're overreacting. I'm sure of it." He walked toward me, lowered his voice. "You're just feeling a little threatened because Adrienne and I were—we used to—"

"Fuck."

He stared at me, appalled. "Jesus."

I stared back: *Prude.*

He shook his head.

"What?" I said. "What were you going to say?"

"I was going to say that Adrienne and I have a past."

A past. How lovely.

"And what a past it is," I said.

He glared at me, lips pursed. "Yes, Elise, we have a past. But Adrienne's not part of my present. Or my future." He paused, took a breath. "You are my present. You are my future. Not her."

"Then why did you invite her here?" I said, tears popping out of the corners of my eyes. "Why did you ask her to have dinner with us? Why did you offer to cook for her when you never cook for me?"

"Because she's moving here and doesn't know anyone except for me. Because she doesn't make friends easily. Because she just broke up with her boyfriend. Because she wanted to see the dog. Because I felt sorry for her."

It seemed ridiculous, unimaginable, to feel sorry for a woman as gorgeous and enviable as Adrienne was. Weren't there far worthier, needier candidates for sympathy? Like me?

"Looks aren't everything, you know. She's not as confident as she seems."

Unlike me. The most confident woman in the world. Snooping and spying and rooting around in every drawer, pocket, and crevice.

"Is that why you two split up? Because she was too needy?"

"It was never going to work with Adrienne and me," he said. "For a lot of reasons."

"Like what?"

"She was a slob. Which I couldn't stand. There were always clothes everywhere."

Lame.

"What else?"

He thought for a moment, then added: "And she was terrible with money. Absolutely terrible. Indulgent. She deprived herself—and me at the time, actually—of nothing."

Better.

"What else?"

"She was very manipulative. She was always finding a way to get her way. Whether it was lying and saying she knew the chef at a particular restaurant so that we'd go where she wanted to go, or completely falling apart into an emotional collapse the few times I put my foot down about something—friends of hers I hated and refused to socialize with; getting to spend at least some holidays with my family, too, instead of just with hers—I could never let my guard down. She was always, always up to something."

Nice.

But now I wanted the real stuff.

"Spill," I said.

He hesitated. "All right, since you really want to know. I knew you'd get it out of me eventually. One of the main reasons Adrienne and I split up was because she didn't want kids. And I did." He shifted his weight uncomfortably. "It was always an issue between us. And I knew it always would be. We had two very different visions of the future, and neither of us was willing to compromise. Not that there is a compromise when it comes to the issue of children. I mean, you either have them or you don't. And having a family was too important to me."

I was quiet, finally.

"Look. Adrienne and I simply weren't meant to be."

I bit the inside of my lip. "Why?"

"Because you and I are meant to be."

"Why?"

"Because," he said, rolling his eyes, like I was one of his annoying ninth graders. "Because I said so."

Chastened, ashamed, pouty, I said nothing. My silence was my apology.

Or so I hoped.

"Now apologize," Donald said.

I shrugged.

"I mean it. Apologize."

I shrugged again.

"Out loud." He leaned against the sink and pulled me toward him; I stared into his chest and played with the buttons of his shirt.

"I'm sorry."

"For?" He stuck his finger under my chin and lifted my head so I would have no place to hide.

"For . . . ?" I had no idea, really.

"For imagining the worst. For your Gloom and Doom. For not believing in me. In us."

I looked into his eyes—clear, guileless, as trusting as a child's—and felt enormous relief. Of course Donald loved me; of course he wasn't going to go back to Adrienne. How crazy was I to have ever thought otherwise.

So I said out loud that I was sorry.

For real, this time.

He nodded. And in that split second, he moved on: forgiving me completely and forgetting the whole episode.

"Now, cut the shit," he said, and turned toward one of the greasy counters. "We have artichokes to butterfly."

15

When Adrienne arrived at eight-fifteen—fashionably late—she couldn't have looked more respectable. Gone were the tight jeans, the low-cut midriff-baring T-shirt, the push-up bra, and in their place was a perfectly simple and very understated (though tight-fitting) ensemble of slate gray trousers and sweater: Jil Sander?

Perfect timing.

Coming into the house and air-kissing her way past me to a full embrace with Donald, she was the picture of sophistication, elegance, and restraint. And sly manipulation (hadn't Donald himself admitted just hours before that she was "always up to something"?).

Donald's eyes pinned me. My reports of Adrienne's sluttiness, it seemed, had been greatly exaggerated. And with that glance, the reassuring effects of the moment we'd had in the kitchen earlier in the afternoon all but disappeared. So much for faith and trust.

Crowded there with the two of them, uncomfortably, in the foyer, inhaling her perfectly delicate perfume (which I recognized: it was, of course, French—Annick Goutal's Eau d'Hadrien—what else?), I hated her guts.

"God, you look fantastic!" Donald effused, taking her in from head to toe. "Really fantastic!"

Adrienne struck a pose. "Do I?" She stepped back an inch or two so Donald could get a better look in order to properly reassure her.

Which he did.

Pavlov's dog redux.

"Oh yes! Really! Fantastic!" He sounded giddy. Clearly, he was having trouble forming complete sentences. It wasn't every day that such a hot number was in his foyer, looking to reconnect with him.

"Thanks." She smiled. *Of course I look fantastic.* And then she added: "So do you."

Surprised, and thrilled, I knew, by the compliment—*he looked fantastic too!*—and always in search of feedback about his physical appearance, Donald stopped short, ran his hands over his cashmere-sweatered chest, hips, stomach, abdomen.

"Really?"

I could've sworn I saw her wink.

Donald ran his hands over himself again, just to be sure. "Well, I do work at it. I watch what I eat. I exercise regularly—every day, in fact. Actually, yesterday I did a full hour on the Stair-Master." Nervously, he looked in my direction and saw the expression on my face: excruciating boredom. "Sorry. Elise hates when I talk about my weight."

I was annoyed. Though it probably was not his intention, he was casting me in the role of the unsupportive woman, the sort of unsympathetic shrew who would, years from now (or, at this rate, months from now), provoke him to whisper to any girl half my age who would listen, "My wife doesn't understand me." And though all attempts would undoubtedly be futile, I knew I had to at least try to defend myself.

"I do not," I said.

"Yes you do."

"I do not!"

"You do so!"

We were like three-year-olds bickering in front of the babysitter.

Donald turned, then, to Adrienne. "And I don't blame her, since I talk about it all the time. I'm kind of neurotic about my weight, in case you hadn't noticed."

Kind of?

"Kind of?" Adrienne said, echoing my inner thoughts. "You've always been more than a little obsessed with your weight."

Donald blushed.

She smiled, grabbed his arm. I had a hunch there would be a quick trip down memory lane. "Remember that time you bought three scales in one week? Because you were convinced that each one was wrong?"

"Well, they *were* wrong," Donald said, a cloud of seriousness drifting over his face as if the event they were discussing had happened yesterday instead of more than several years ago. "I mean, I did not weigh two hundred and thirty-three pounds."

"Of course you didn't," she reassured.

"I mean, it was a physical impossibility."

"Of course it was."

"There are linebackers in the NFL who don't weigh two hundred and thirty-three pounds."

"I know."

"Which is why that whole incident at the doctor's office wasn't my fault."

I shifted uncomfortably, waiting for someone to fill me in.

Adrienne turned to me. "He went for a checkup, and as part of his routine physical exam, the nurse weighed him."

He glared at me, reliving the moment of horror, humiliation. "Two thirty-three. I told her that that was impossible. That their scale was incorrect."

"But they insisted that their scale was accurate, because they were using one of those doctor's scales with the weights. Apparently, they're never wrong."

"Never say never," he said.

They both paused for a second or two, trying to figure out which one of them should continue. I sensed there was more to the story. Which of course there was.

"Donald had kind of a meltdown," Adrienne said.

"I went crazy."

I knew instantly what was coming.

"He pulled his pants down."

He nodded proudly, as if he had performed a grand act of civil disobedience.

"Not only did I pull my pants down," he said. "But I—"

"He got down on all fours."

My God.

"Yes! I did! In protest! I got down on all fours and I said: 'This is an injustice! I will not accept this! I will not allow an incorrect weight to be recorded in my medical file!' "

I blinked, wondering what I was getting myself into. *Was he insane?*

"So they changed it," he said.

I wasn't surprised. "To what?" I asked.

"Two twenty-two. Which is what I'm sure I was."

We all took a breath; collected ourselves; tried to move on and resume a less mad course of conversation.

"Anyway," he said, turning back to Adrienne. "How long has it been?"

She sighed wistfully. "A long time," she said. "Too long."

Not long enough.

"Was it two years ago?"

She ran her tongue over her teeth. "Yes. I think so."

"In New York. Right before I moved here."

"I remember now." She paused nostalgically. "You had some books of mine."

"All your Proust. And all those goddamn Russians."

She smiled smugly. "It was just a few volumes."

"Are you kidding? It was an entire library! I think you've read every Dostoyevsky translation there is."

"Well, not every."

"Most, then."

She lowered her eyes demurely.

"Anyway, there were, for several months after you moved out, two huge boxes left in the back of my closet. I had no room for my shoes!"

"Maybe if you didn't have so many shoes you'd have had room for them."

"I am kind of a clotheshorse," he said. "In case you haven't noticed."

He was the only teacher at Sidwell who wore Brooks Brothers jackets, Zegna ties; Barneys shoes; perfect rimless eyeglasses expertly selected and hand-fitted by Jamie at Robert Marc on Madison Avenue. All wardrobe leftovers from his past life in finance.

"And so are you!" Donald said to Adrienne.

She looked down at her outfit, then shrugged helplessly. A victim of literature *and* fashion.

"And then," he continued, "there were the photographs."

Photographs?

I stopped cold.

Of what? Whom? When? Where?

Were they more summer-vacation beach pictures?

Happy-relationship pictures?

And though I couldn't imagine Donald engaging in anything of the sort, I still had to ask myself the unthinkable:

Were they erotic pictures?

The Evil Twins—obsessional snooping and insane jealousy— reared their ugly heads like rabid gophers. They whispered bad thoughts, barked orders in my head: *find those photographs*. I tried to ignore them, but the possibilities—the compulsion to find out as much as I could about Adrienne and about her past with Donald; the dread and misery attached to the finding out; the fear of what I would learn—made me shaky.

After a few more minutes of small talk in the foyer, during

which time some part of Adrienne's body never left some part of Donald's, she looked at him with great excitement and grabbed his arm again.

"So where *is* she?"

Donald looked confused. "She's here," he said, turning her around to see me. "Right here."

Adrienne's face fell. "No," she said, looking back up at Donald with her big brown eyes. "I meant Lucy. Where's Lucy?"

Donald tried to engage me in the contagion of his nervous laughing fit, but I would have none of it. "Of course!" he continued, too loudly and clearly rattled, his hands flying around and gesticulating wildly.

I smiled sharply, falsely. So did Adrienne.

"You mean *Lucy!*" he said. "The *dog!*"

More smiling.

More wincing.

I kicked Donald.

Where the fuck was the dog already?

"Well, actually," he said, "she's outside. Elise gets kind of annoyed when the dog is in the kitchen and we're cooking."

Here we go again.

"I do not."

I did.

"Yes you do."

"I do *not.*"

"Yes you do. And I don't blame you." Again, he turned toward Adrienne. "I mean, of course I don't blame her. Lucy is terrible. She's always begging for food and manipulating her way into a meal." He started to laugh again. "I mean, she's just terrible, isn't she? You remember, right?"

Adrienne laughed too. "Remember when she started eating so much that we thought there might be something physically wrong with her? Like maybe she had a tapeworm?"

"No. You thought she had something *psychologically* wrong with her." He turned to me for the punch line. "Adrienne thought Lucy had an eating disorder!"

"I did not."

He continued to make his case to me. "Oh, I quite assure you. Adrienne thought Lucy had an eating disorder. A new form of bulimia! Binging without the purging."

These two really were crazy.

"Maybe she was pregnant," I threw in, just as a lark.

They both turned to me, as if I were clairvoyant. "How did you know?" they said in unison.

Lucky thing I'd edited *Improving Your Pet's Sex Life* and *The High-Protein Low-Fat No-Carb Pet Diet* the previous year.

"She had six puppies," Adrienne said. "Six incredibly big, healthy, strong puppies. Which the vet was convinced was because of the prenatal vitamins Donald made sure she took."

"There are prenatal vitamins for dogs?" I asked, incredulous, not really wanting to know the answer.

"No, actually. I just made them myself. I'd grind up a whole bunch of different vitamins in the Cuisinart. That way she didn't have to swallow a mouthful of giant horse pills."

And he wondered why I was sometimes jealous of his dog? Why, at the beginning of our courtship, when he'd yell something out from the kitchen—*"Want a cookie?"; "Come in here!"; "Sit!"; "Out!"*—I would answer; obey? He could never understand why I thought he was talking to me and not the dog, but I thought it was obvious: Lucy was someone Donald trusted, felt very close to, connected with.

Once again, finally, we came back to the present.

There was more smiling.

More wincing.

I kicked Donald again.

The dog?

"Oh sorry. I put her outside when I started cooking, which was"—he checked his watch—"at one? Or two, maybe? And now it's eight?"

Adrienne expressed concern. "She's probably starving."

"And lonely," he added.

And half-frozen. The Evil Twins were out of control; wreaking havoc; filled with glee at the idea of the dog's discomfort.

Donald led the way through the foyer into the kitchen as if he were leading an emergency life-or-death dog-saving expedition across the tundra. We both followed. He took the key to the back door from the top of the refrigerator, grabbed the platter of swordfish steaks and vegetables to be grilled, then raced across the kitchen and unlocked the door. They both ran out into the yard. Barking and laughing ensued.

I was in desperate need of a drink. I took a giant swig of white wine from an open bottle in the refrigerator, wiped my mouth with the back of my arm, took another swig, and finished the bottle. I exhaled loudly, belched daintily, then heard the doorbell and went to the door: Gayle.

"Oh. It's you," I said.

"Yes, it's me."

"Drink?" I looked at the empty bottle still in my hand. "I was just going to open more."

"Yes, *please*." Her tone was that of someone who hadn't been fed in days. She followed me into the kitchen and looked around longingly at the dinner in progress. Momentarily distracted by all that food and the prospect of a fantastic meal, she soon caught herself and dug her fingers into my arm.

"So. Is she here yet?"

I slammed the bottle of wine I was trying to open down onto the counter. "Look, do *not* start with me again. I'm not in the mood."

She blinked madly. "Start what?"

"You know what. That Adrienne bullshit. '*Oh, is she here? Where is she? I'm dying to see my new best friend Adrienne!*'" I mimicked. "Of course she's here. She's outside with Donald, playing with the dog." I finally pulled the cork out of the bottle, wiped the inside of the bottle neck with my finger, then poured a glass for Gayle. I handed it to her, turned back to the counter, and drank another long swig from the bottle.

"What are you doing?" Gayle asked.

"I'm drinking."

"From the bottle, yes I see. How lovely." She took a sip from her glass, put it down, assessed the scene before her. "Look. You'd better pull yourself together, here."

I felt another belch coming on, but I squelched it.

"What do you mean?"

"That woman is outside with your fiancé—her ex-fiancé. She's here, in your home, about to sit down at your premarital dinner table, and you had better not be drunk. Do you follow?"

"I'd say I had better not be *sober*," I lobbed back.

She was not amused. "I said, Do you follow?"

I arched an eyebrow.

"Well," she went on, despite my eyebrow. "You had better follow. You need your wits about you tonight. Your wits and all your faculties. Because if you don't think she's here to make trouble, then you know nothing about women and how they work."

"And you do?"

She paused awkwardly. "Well, no. Not really. Not when it comes to my own life." I remembered, in a flash, the stories Gayle had told me about her ex-husbands and ex-boyfriends; how common sense and suspiciousness always disappeared the minute she fell in love. "But I think I'm very sharp when it comes to other people's lives. Like yours." She looked at me, grabbed at a corner of my sweater. I hadn't had time to change since I'd returned, and figured I'd just wear the sweater for dinner, too (did I feel, subconsciously, an urge to get my money's worth at least?). "Which is why you should change into something a little more seductive."

I couldn't believe what I was hearing. "Excuse me?"

"Something slightly provocative. Sexy. Or at least more revealing than that body-covering sweater."

Feeling as vulnerable as I did, the last thing I felt like doing was exposing any more of myself than I absolutely had to.

"If you think you're so sharp," I said, stalling for time, "then why did you make such a scene today? You were all over her! Fawning and drooling."

"No I wasn't!" She reached for her glass, probably trying to buy herself enough time to come up with an excuse.

"Yes you were. You blew it today for me. You sided with Adrienne. Not only did I lose face, but I lost my footing." I stopped a minute, considered the great disadvantage I was in because of that. "I was relying on you to keep me centered." I didn't have an excess of confidence to begin with, but I could usually bluff a good game. And now I couldn't even do that.

"God, I'm sorry you see it that way, Elise."

"You should be sorry."

"It's just that I became rather caught up in the excitement of the day. The airport, the fancy lunch, the shopping, and the sight of her waiting on the curb with that fantastic coat—"

"There you go again!" I closed my eyes, leaned against the counter, tried to focus. I could smell the fish grilling outside. Time for talking and strategizing was running out. "So, do you really think she wants to get him back?"

"I'm not sure, but clearly she wants something. You don't come off a plane looking like that if you intend to live and let live."

I swallowed. She'd just confirmed my darkest suspicions.

"Now, that said," she continued, "it's lucky Donald doesn't go in for that kind of thing."

"What kind of thing? Flirting?" Because there had been plenty of that already. I thought about the last twenty minutes in the foyer.

"No. That low-cut aggressively sexual way of dressing. I mean, the minute he saw that tonight he was probably completely turned off. Am I right?"

My heart sank, though I was momentarily reassured by the correctness of Gayle's observations, for it was true that Donald didn't go for that way of dressing. If only Adrienne was still dressed the way she had been earlier today, we would have a slightly different situation on our hands. "She changed her clothes," I said glumly.

"No!"

"Oh yes."

"To what?"

I described her new, more somber outfit. "Jesus, Gayle. It's like Dr. Jekyll and—"

"Mrs. Hyde. Or rather, *Miss* Hyde who hopes to *become* Mrs. Hyde."

"Thanks," I said. "Thanks for further underscoring that fact. If I didn't already feel completely despondent about the situation, I do now."

"Look. Listen." Her long, delicate neck tightened as she searched for a way to spin something positive out of my troublesome circumstances. But just as she started to open her mouth, the doorbell rang.

"Who's that?" she asked.

"It's Terrance. He's a friend of Donald's. From school. I met him once and he's cute. He teaches history and coaches girls' soccer and basketball. I thought it would be a good idea to invite him—you know, like a fix-up. So Adrienne would have someone to date when she moves down here. So she'd have someone else to focus on besides Donald."

"A discreet sort of off-loading! What a brilliant plan!" Gayle nodded at me as if we were in a James Bond movie.

"It's not a *brilliant* plan. It's just a plan. A desperate plan, even. Anything to contain the potential threat that . . . that *person's* moving here poses for me—for us!"

I moved toward the front of the house and opened the door. The answer to my prayers—Terrance Cafferty, tall, lean, sandy-haired, innocent—stood there in his tweed jacket and Oxford cloth shirt, looking very, well, *potential.* Though I'd only met him twice before (once at a school cocktail party fund-raiser; another time at a home basketball game with Donald), I threw my arms around him, thanked him too profusely for coming, and grabbed the bottle of wine he had so politely brought along. Then I took his hand and led him into the kitchen.

Introducing him to Gayle, I offered, then poured, him a drink. Orange juice is what he asked for: a bad sign, I thought, given the probability of Adrienne's extremely sophisticated palate for wine (she wouldn't give a non–*vin* drinker the *heure du jour,* I assumed). He was thirsty, he said, after coaching that afternoon's Saturday game. They'd lost, which was another concern: Adrienne, I was certain, only liked winners. After I extracted a promise from him that he would absolutely have a glass of something— "anything alcoholic"—later at dinner, I pointed at the screen door to the backyard.

"Donald's out there with Lucy, the dog," I said, then hiccuped.

Terrance nodded. "I didn't know Donald had a dog."

"Yes, well, he does. It was the dog he and Adrienne had when they were together. He got custody of the dog after he dumped her."

Terrance sipped his juice. "I thought *she* broke it off. At least, that's what he told me."

I froze. Donald had always told me that he had ended it. Adrienne had wanted different things (money, power, a big chunk of prime Manhattan real estate) than he did (peace, quiet, a house with a yard, kids); she expected too much from him (everything); they could never agree on anything (she was always right, he was always wrong). For the second time that day, I'd caught him in a lie—an untruth, to be generous, which I didn't particularly feel like being—and I was reeling. It didn't take long to know, suddenly, with complete certainty, that I was in over my head. Adrienne was far too much for me; I would never survive this, let alone win.

I excused myself to go upstairs, change my clothes, freshen my makeup. Gayle was right: on the way, I poured myself a tall glass of water. I decided to sober up. Fast. I needed my wits about me. Such as they were.

In time, Donald and Adrienne came back inside with the dog and the serving platter heaping with swordfish and vegetables. A blast of cold late-November air gusted into the kitchen before they shut the door behind them. The topic of conversation was being finished off: the fact that Adrienne wished she could have joint custody of Lucy when she moved to Washington.

"But, as I tried to remind her," Donald said, looking my way to include me, "she won't be able to have a dog at the Kennedy-Warren apartment building."

Disappointment and tragic sadness registered on everyone's face. And then:

Introductions were made (Adrienne and Terrance), hands were shaken (Adrienne and Terrance); cheeks were kissed (Adrienne and Gayle; Gayle and Donald); dinner was served. Sitting down in the dining room with our glorious grilled meal of horseradish-crusted swordfish steaks, butterflied artichokes, and passing the bread and shallow plates of olive oil for dipping and a simple arugula and shaved Parmesan salad (Adrienne opted out of serving herself greens at that point in the meal, by the way: she was, she explained, accustomed to the "Continental" habit of having her salad at the *end*), it would have looked, to any outside observer who didn't know any better, as if we were a wonderfully warm group of interesting people who wished each other well.

But of course, that's not what we were at all.

Not Adrienne and me, anyway.

We were competitors in the oldest competition in the book: passive-aggressively, tacitly, unofficially, *we were fighting over a man*. The thought that I was engaged in such a banal, politically incorrect endeavor depressed me greatly. Never before had I overtly competed with another woman for anything—let alone a man. Never before had I viewed another woman as the Enemy. Had I always had great girlfriends, or had I simply been too naive all these years to see them as adversaries? Or was it because, until now, I hadn't had someone worth fighting for and someone I was forced to fight for? This was a game I could not forfeit. And so, regarding Donald across the table (his charmingly tousled hair; his flushed cheeks; his strong smooth neck coming out of the V neck of his black cashmere sweater), I pledged to myself that I would see this through to the end, whatever that was, wherever it took me.

Unfortunately, however, my resolve was not (I thought of the overdue manuscript on my desk and nearly laughed bitterly out loud) "empowering," "enhancing," or "ennobling."

I was suffering, in silence, barely eating a thing (I had the fat hangover, still, from that afternoon of watching Adrienne try on clothes), keeping away from the (fishy-smelling) fish and only picking at the artichokes and salad; I had my greens *with* the meal, thank you very much. And all the while, the fix-up with Adrienne and Terrance was going nicely. (Big surprise. Did anything *not* go well for Adrienne?) He was, of course, looking at her with huge, wet eyes, his mouth hanging open a little. But she barely noticed that aspect of his aspect. I assumed it was because any man who had ever seen her, sat with her, watched her get out of a car or sit down at a restaurant, shared a meal with her, had sex with her, or simply existed for any amount of time in the same general vicinity with her must have eventually exhibited the identical involuntary pathetic look of quiet desperation:

I love you.

Much was made of Adrienne's impending move from Manhattan, her challenging new job at the National Gallery, and the rather extraordinary digs at the Kennedy-Warren she would soon be moving into, with Adrienne and Gayle regaling the table with anecdotes from the day in antiphony. First, Adrienne would describe something (*"The apartment is big"*). Then, Gayle would breathlessly embellish it (*"The apartment is simply the biggest and most gorgeous flat I have ever seen in my whole life!"*).

Terrance swooned. Donald was riveted.

I excused myself and left the room.

Wandering into the kitchen, pretending to be in desperate search of something I desperately needed (A butcher knife? A shotgun? Liquid arsenic which I could guzzle straight from the bottle?), I paced from stove to refrigerator to pantry and back again, still ruminating about why Adrienne unhinged me so.

Whatever her intentions were (and I was sure they were not good), did I really think Donald would leave me?

Sort of.

Did I really think he wanted her back?

Maybe.

Was I so insecure about our relationship and about love in general that I could imagine us so easily coming apart at the seams?

Apparently so.

After all, technically, despite what Donald had told me earlier that afternoon—which I phrased to myself now as: Adrienne is a slob and a spendthrift with no maternal instincts—he'd never said anything about not having feelings for her anymore.

Listening to the voices wafting in from the other room, I could hear Adrienne bantering back and forth with Donald (about what I couldn't hear, but the tone of her voice was unmistakable) and flirting lightly—dallying, to be precise—with poor Terrance. And I could just imagine the mental calculations taking place in her head:

Terrance was sweet enough. Smart enough. Attractive enough. But not rich enough. Not interesting enough. Not substantial enough. And it was then that I suddenly realized what it all, ultimately, added up to:

Terrance was a lightweight. A cat toy. She would paw him around the floor for a while until she got bored.

Kicking myself for not having figured that out before we'd fixed them up, and bemoaning the fact that nothing I had done since Adrienne had stepped off that plane had gone right—not Gayle, not Fran, and now, not Terrance—I saw my amateur, bush-league machinations backfiring. I was in a tailspin—a death spin, as pilots call it.

I reentered the dining room just as Donald was going into the kitchen. *Ships passing in the night*, I thought melodramatically, fatalistically (it was all that wine on a still empty stomach). He kissed me on the cheek and then disappeared to bring out our dessert: pears poached in Armagnac. When he returned with them and we were both reseated, all eyes turned again toward Adrienne.

". . . It's not something I generally like to talk about," she was murmuring (audibly enough, though, to be overheard) to Gayle. "But it's part of who I am, I guess."

As always, my curiosity got the better of me. I took the bait, asked her what she was talking about.

She smiled demurely, flipped the hair away from her face, and once again removed one pesky strand that had gotten stuck in her lip gloss. I looked over at Donald to see if he knew what was coming, but his face was a blank. We were entering uncharted territory. I wondered quickly if she was going to start name-dropping again.

"My father is a scientist. A molecular biologist. He's a professor—head of the department, actually—at Yale medical school."

Gayle, who had been eating her poached pear with such velocity and intensity as not to be believed, suddenly choked on a mouthful. Accepting a slap on the back from Donald and a refill to her water glass from Terrance, she still managed somehow to wave her hand in Adrienne's direction, imploring her to continue. Which, of course, she did.

"Anyway," she resumed, "my father is the pathologist who studied Einstein's brain. To see if there were any clues to his genius."

There was a hushed silence. Which I felt compelled to break.

"His actual brain?" I said, knowing I asked the question for the whole table.

"Yes. He sectioned Einstein's brain to determine whether there were significant quantifiable physical differences between it and a normal brain."

Forks dropped. Lips were licked, re-licked. Then, a barrage of questions directed at Adrienne immediately erupted: *Had she ever seen the brain herself?* (No.) *Had her father known Einstein when he was alive?* (No.) *Were there indeed quantifiable physical differences between Einstein's brain and a normal brain?* (No.)

The table was mesmerized. I could have taken all my clothes off and set myself on fire and nobody would have noticed.

Her father had fondled Einstein's brain? Her mother knew Dries Van Noten? Ben Bradlee was her godfather?

I sat back and let the discussion continue for another few minutes, desperate to figure out a way to stick a pin in all the excitement. Suddenly, a factoid I'd happened upon in a manuscript and remembered for no apparent reason came to me in a flash of absolute brilliance:

"You know, I read that when they autopsied Secretariat, they found that his heart was two and a half times the size of a normal horse's heart."

Four sets of eyeballs turned to me and blinked. Not a word was spoken. A second or two passed out of respect for my *grand mal* seizure of idiocy, I suppose, before they all turned back to Adrienne for another fifteen minutes of unbridled infatuation.

When things finally settled down, when the pears had been devoured, the coffee served and finished, Adrienne yawned. A big, luxuriously sensual yawn; the giant cat, spent. All movement and conversation immediately ceased.

"I'm *exhausted*," she purred. "I really must go."

Terrance practically exploded as he offered—panting, sweating, his life depending on her answer—to drive her back to her hotel.

"All right." *I'll let you.*

At which point he leapt from the table and retrieved their coats from the hall closet as fast as he could, before she had time to change her mind.

Adrienne looked over at Donald, who was (as he did after every meal) feeling his (nonexistent) fat. I knew she was trying to gauge his jealousy level. Had he heard her agree to Terrance's offer? Apparently not. So consumed was he by his own physique that he seemed not to notice a thing. So when Terrance brought her coat and stood next to her at the ready to help her on with it, she stretched languidly and leaned into him.

"Perhaps we could have a nightcap," she said seductively. "There's a lovely bar at the hotel."

How subtle.

Donald looked up distractedly.

"Which hotel is that?" he asked, suddenly interested. His hands continued to run absently over his soft (fatless) folds of cashmere.

"The Jefferson. Terrance is going to drop me there and stay for a drink." She held his arm and snuggled into him.

He smiled, swooned.

(Poor Terrance. He would never know what hit him.)

Donald shifted in his seat, glanced up at Adrienne and then over at Terrance. "Great." His voice was flat. "And you're off early tomorrow on the shuttle?"

She eyed her witless accomplice. "Maybe I'll sleep in, take my time getting back." She flipped her hair again demurely, and inched Terrance toward the door.

We followed.

And Gayle, not wanting to be left behind, lunged for her coat in the closet.

"It was a wonderful dinner," Adrienne whispered into Donald's ear as she leaned across to plant a kiss on his cheek. "And Elise—" She looked toward me and through me. "Elise is *lovely.*"

Donald smiled proudly, and pulled me toward him with a strong arm.

"Yes she is, isn't she? She's the love of my life." He kissed me tenderly then on the neck as if he really meant it, and for the first time that day—actually, for the first time since Adrienne had called the week before and my nightmare began—all my inner demons, the Quartet of Jewish Gloom and Doom, the Evil Twins, were quieted.

Adrienne flinched ever so slightly. "And I can see why."

And with that last comment, she exited our home with Terrance in tow and Gayle following close behind, trying to chase the tail of her comet.

The house was quiet; the dog asleep. Donald and I walked back to the kitchen and sat among the ruins—the plates were stacked on the counter, lined up and ready to be loaded into the dishwasher; pots and pans and serving platters and grill racks waited to be scrubbed. I turned to him in the dim light. A broad, relaxed smile spread across his face.

"Well, I think that went very well," he said.

"Yes."

A lie.

"The fish was great."

"Yes."

"And the vegetables?"

"Grilled to perfection."

The vegetables sucked, I thought. Burnt, charred, reeking of gas.

"And Terrance and Adrienne. They really seemed to hit it off. I wonder if they'll—you know," he said, "get together."

"You mean, tonight? In the hotel? As in, have sex?"

He shook his head. "No, no. Adrienne would never do that. She has a strict rule about that: five dates."

"Is that how long she waited before sleeping with you?"

Donald blanched. "What?"

"Is that how long she waited? Or, should I say, is that how long she made you wait? Back when you first met her?"

"I don't quite know where you're going with this."

"Okay. Let me be more blunt: You and Adrienne were having quite a love fest all night."

"What are you talking about?"

"You heard me. You were having a love fest. A flirt fest. A great time reminiscing and retelling all your charming little romantic stories."

"Elise," he said wearily, "we were not having a love fest. We were just—"

"Just what? Reconnecting?"

He considered the statement. "Well, actually, yes. That's exactly what we were doing. We hadn't seen each other for two years. We were just catching up."

"Bullshit. You were flirting."

"I was not."

"You were so."

"Elise! Honey!" He tried to make this all sound silly and inconsequential. "I was not flirting! I was just, you know, excited to see her. And nervous."

"Excited? And nervous?" I put my hands out in front of me like two sides of a scale. "Sounds like flirting to me."

He shrugged, with just a trace of guilt. "Okay. So maybe I was being a little too"—he stopped, tried to search for the most accurate, least incriminating word (as far as I was concerned, one didn't exist)—"friendly."

"The only one drooling more than you was Lucy. And the only one drooling more than Lucy was Terrance. And he had an excuse."

"Which was?"

"He's a guy. A single guy. And he was being fixed up with her."

"Well I'm a guy, too!" He shrugged, as if he were blameless, a victim of his own gender. "And, if I may speak frankly for a moment, when you're a guy, and you're in the presence of two very attractive women—one of whom is your fiancée and the other of whom used to be your fiancée—well, it can get a little overwhelming."

"Overwhelming?"

"Confusing." He was digging his hole now with two shovels.

"Well that's reassuring. That you're overwhelmed with confusion."

"That's not what I said. That's not what I meant."

I stared at him, decided to keep going while I had the chance. "So if Adrienne and Terrance get involved—start dating—when she moves here, will it bother you? Overwhelm you with confusion?"

"Of course not. I mean, that's why we invited him, isn't it? So that she could have someone to go out with socially. She doesn't know a soul here, she said."

Right. Mary Tyler Moore making her way in the big city.

Adrienne didn't know a soul, except for Donald, and me, and now Gayle and Fran and Terrance.

"So you won't get jealous."

"Jealous? Absolutely not."

"Really." I rolled my eyes. "I find that very hard to believe."

"Look." Donald slammed one hand down on the counter, then ran the other hand through his hair. It seemed he'd finally had enough of this line of questioning from which no good would ever come: there was only so long you could get sucked into a discussion about your ex without inadvertently stepping on a mine field. He knew it was only a matter of time (minutes; seconds) before the whole thing really blew up in his face; he had to shut me down now. "Our relationship, hers and mine, was a long time ago. A very long time ago. I only wish the best for her. I only want her to be happy."

I looked at him, suspicious of his magnanimity. "Why?"

"Because. The happier she is, the happier we are."

I said nothing.

"Am I right?"

I shrugged.

He looked at me, took my hand, held it. "I'm marrying you. Not her. Right?"

I didn't answer.

"You're the one I love. Not her. Okay?"

Still nothing.

"So can we just go to bed now and forget all about this? I'm exhausted. And I think I ate too much." He ran his hands over his torso one last time; put his arm around me; looked worried. "Do you think my weight will go up?"

I rested my head against his chest; closed my eyes for a few brief seconds. His heart beat beneath his sweater, slowly, steadily into my ear. At that particular moment, there was something oddly comforting about the question. It was familiar; intimate; the fact that he'd asked it implied that everything between us was still certain, that nothing had changed.

We shut the lights off and climbed the stairs in the dark, leaving the kitchen's mess until morning. Yet as we did, I could almost feel a change in air pressure:

Those Evil Twins; that old Gloom and Doom—they were all back, lurking in the shadows again.

16

That Monday morning, after Adrienne had gone back to New York and Donald back to school, everything should have returned to normal. Only it didn't. Sitting motionless at the kitchen table, I tried to take Gayle's advice and start focusing on my life with Donald again.

Not on his past life with Adrienne. Or our upcoming future with her here. But it wasn't easy.

Having wasted so much time preparing for and enduring Adrienne's first visit, and having wasted so much money, too—the French beauty treatments alone were enough to set me back several thousand francs, not to mention that sweater—I was now very behind on our wedding plans. Yet the thought of trying to play catch-up seemed beyond me. I felt as if a bomb had gone off in my backyard over the weekend. How was I supposed to think of stupid flower arrangements at a time like this?

I drank cup after cup of coffee and ate countless miniature Reese's cups from Donald's secret stash; replayed scenes from the weekend; assessed the damage. All the while wondering: *Whose idea was it to have a wedding in the first place?*

Not mine, in fact.

I thought back.

Donald had proposed to me one night last July in the living room after a perfect dinner (he always got especially romantic following a fabulous—and fabulously expensive—meal) down the street at Palena. We'd each had the three-course tasting menu: house-cured smoked salmon topped with chopped greens and hazelnuts to start; veal chop with paprika sauce; chocolate mousse and French-pressed coffee for dessert—a selection Donald recently said he wished we could replicate for the reception. Down on both knees—he was so tall otherwise, and balancing on one knee was far too complicated for him at a moment like that, he'd told me later—holding out that beautiful Tiffany-blue box with the perfect little midnight-blue velvet box inside, to my shock and amazement, he'd asked.

I'd said yes.

Joyous, disbelieving, his eyes filled with tears.

My head started spinning: *We were getting married*. And in my ecstatic, excited stupor, as we called our families to tell them the news and quickly refused their seemingly generous offers to help plan (interfere with) and pay for (control) the wedding—we were, after all, adults, we felt, and should plan and pay for it ourselves— I'd simply assumed we'd have something small; a Justice of the Peace; a handful of friends and relatives; perhaps a cocktail party or dinner afterwards to accommodate a slightly larger group of celebrants. I'd assumed that we (Donald at thirty-eight and me at thirty-four; survivors, between the two of us, of nearly eight decades of failed relationships, dashed hopes, aborted dreams), were beyond all that, all the silly nuptial festivities; all the customs and ceremony and ritual; all the tulle and lace and silk and satin.

But I was wrong.

Donald was not beyond all that.

He wanted the pomp, the circumstance, the bells, the whistles.

"So you want to make a public spectacle of our union," I said sadly, the next morning over coffee at Politics and Prose.

"Weddings are meant to be celebrations," he'd argued, looking at me as if I were some incredibly rare species that should be caged and put on display: *a woman who did not want a big wedding*. "They're meant to be witnessed. All throughout history, throughout every culture, weddings are festive events attended by hordes of friends and family. That is the way of humanity. That is the way of the world."

I frowned. I could not imagine a bachelor party; interfaith-marriage religious counseling; walking down the aisle together: me, a full foot shorter than Donald; Donald surely bumping his head on low-hanging trellises, flowers, light fixtures, *chuppah*, if there was one. I tried to explain my superficial misgivings, but he would have none of it.

I didn't blame him.

"I don't buy it," he said, searching my eyes for the truth. "Now tell me the real reason you don't want a wedding."

I wished I could have, but it was all too difficult to articulate; impossible to justify. That to me, big weddings with guests and dresses and rented tuxedos and flowers and bands and buffet food stations were for other people. For people who had faith in the future of their happiness; who did not see such a festive event as tempting fate, as an absolute precursor to divorce. So I just said this:

"Weddings scare me."

And thinking that meant I had a sort of stage fright—a fear of public displays of affection—he scooped me up in his arms and dismissed my fear unilaterally.

"There's nothing to be afraid of!" he said, as if he knew already just how dark were the depths of negativity in the woman who had just agreed to marry him. "I'll be with you the whole time!"

I fought the impulse to succumb to my usual pessimism. Instead, moved by Donald's touching effort to always understand me even when I didn't understand myself, I grabbed his hand, held it tightly to my forehead like a cool compress and closed my eyes.

Then I excused myself and went next door to the CVS and bought twenty pounds of bridal magazines to try to get myself in the mood.

But that was months ago.

Worlds ago.

The matrimonial wheels were set in motion, now; there was no going back.

Our deposits, for one thing, would not be returned; all our hordes of friends and family, for another, were expecting invitations, not cancellations.

And so, in the weeks that followed Adrienne's visit, I turned inward; forged ahead. I called, faxed, emailed, decided, finalized, confirmed, wrote checks.

Of course, all of this nose-to-the-grindstone business had to be negotiated, and then cleared, with the Evil Twins. With the specter of Adrienne lingering in the house (her French perfume; the moping, lovesick dog who seemed to have no more use for me since being reunited with her true mistress) and the "souvenir" of her visit I'd managed to save—a white cloth napkin she'd used at dinner and which held, like a fly in amber, a perfectly preserved smudge of her stunning lipstick, which I simply had to have (I planned on taking the napkin with me to Saks, or Neiman's, or even to Barneys in New York if I had to, in a quasi-forensic quest to try to match it), the Twins were on high alert for intelligence. Their insatiable need for information would have to be met, I knew. With my back up against the wall, in complete desperation, I struck a deal with their lidless ids:

Once the wedding planning work was done, the spying shenanigans could resume with a vengeance.

They agreed: since Adrienne hadn't even moved yet, we wouldn't really be missing much anyway.

17

Adrienne's move was scheduled to take place on Saturday, January fifteenth, but don't think for a second that just because she hadn't arrived yet she was out of sight or out of mind.

Every few days or so after she left our dinner table that late November evening, and with the alarming unpredictability of an inflicter of random violence (no set pattern could be established for when she would call, and why), she would leave a message for us on our answering machine:

"Hi Donald. Hi Elise. It's Adrienne," each message would begin, as if we were one big happy *ménage à trois*. Then she would proceed to either ask a favor (*"Could either of you possibly be able to let the phone people into my apartment on . . . ?"*), impart information (*"My moving date has been pushed up a day to Friday, January fourteenth . . . "*), or, in my opinion, simply torture (*"It won't be long now: only six more weeks . . . !"*). If she ever managed to get Donald on the phone, I never knew about it. Which began to make me suspicious:

Were these innocuous messages really that innocent? Were they a smoke screen, containing coded instructions for scheduling phone dates, romantic trysts? Was she calling him — and reaching him — privately on his cell phone? Were they having long, secret, nostalgic conversations full of sadness and regret about the dog, about New York, about the past which I knew nothing about?

Initial investigations into these variations of the same question turned up nothing. As I had done in the past, after Donald would fall asleep, I'd creep downstairs to his study and snoop. Only now, my techniques for infiltration were a little more sophisticated. I'd find his cell phone, press the automatic voicemail retrieval button on the keypad (he had programmed it so his access code and password didn't have to be reentered every time), and scroll through the list of incoming calls he'd received. Then, with the slim metal phone pressed to my ear, my heart pounding with guilt, I'd listen to any messages he had received or saved. But they were all unincriminating: the dry cleaner calling about shirts he'd forgotten to pick up; a school administrator scheduling an English department meeting; a parent thanking him for giving a child another chance on a pop quiz. Tiptoeing back up the stairs afterwards, I couldn't help feeling incredibly foolish: every time I looked, I found nothing. When would I give up the search?

Never.

No matter how many times an investigative mission came up empty, I never felt relieved or secure.

Because I knew it was only a matter of time before I hit pay dirt.

By early December, just after the first snow had fallen and quieted our already quiet city under a soft layer of white powder, I had ironed out all the details at Dumbarton House (no *chuppah*; a Justice of the Peace in lieu of clergy; a tent); decided on the music (a single violinist for the ceremony; a jazz quartet during the reception); selected a videographer (a friend of a friend of Gayle's) and photographer (formerly of the *Washington Post*; black-and-white shots, predominantly). Anne, a close friend of the writer from the Sunday Styles section of the *New York Times* who shows up at weddings and reports on them as if they were actual news stories, had offered to "pitch" our story—*two ex–New Yorkers who'd actually met on that Northeast Corridor!*—for possible "coverage." But though I knew my mother, an unapologetic addict of *People* magazine, would have loved a publicized wedding, the idea of having some gauzy photo of my predictably Edwardian Peter Fox shoes or Donald's cake-and-frosting covered face next to the "story of us" made me queasy with embarrassment. "Then just make sure there's someone for me to sexually harass at the reception," said Anne when I told her no.

By mid-month the invitations and thank-you notes had been ordered (thermography); a calligrapher hired; rooms at the Tabard Inn for our out-of-town guests secured. By the end of December, Donald's custom-ordered black suit (Armani) had come in and was awaiting alterations, and the hotel room for the wedding night had been reserved (a junior suite at the Hay-Adams, overlooking Lafayette Square, with a view of the White House).

By New Year's Day, after a quiet celebration the night before at home together; a pre-midnight phone call from Adrienne (*"This is going to be a great year for all of us. I just know it!"*), and an hour or so of frantic late-night spying provoked by her phone call (Donald's cell phone, date book, wallet; the pockets of two coats and three pairs of pants; the desktop documents of his computer, which he'd left on), I took stock of our situation. Our wedding plans were in good shape. Considering the fact that I'd been simmering on a low boil for weeks, ready to self-sabotage at any moment.

My to-do list had certainly shrunk, and I felt deserving of a special treat to reward my Herculean efforts.

Jealousy, envy, and obsession returned (not that they'd ever really left).

I welcomed them with open arms.

There was still a great deal to do, though.

There was the menu. And the cake. And the flowers. And the ring. And, of course, there was the little matter of the dress.

But with every pending decision, I couldn't help obsessing about what Adrienne would have selected were this her wedding. Staring at the caterer's eighteen-page fax of menu options (which came in addition to the endless list of options contained in the thick packet of information they'd sent to me in the mail), for instance, I couldn't help wondering:

Would Adrienne serve lobster thermidor? Leg of lamb? A chateaubriand? Or a grilled salmon? Dover sole? Trout almandine?

Would her cake be multitiered? Buttercream? Chocolate? Yellow? Or mocha-raspberry-mousse-filled? Or would she instead have the traditional French wedding cake, a croquembouche?

My curiosity expanded like a mushroom cloud; other questions arose.

Looking at the lists of flowers and gemstones to choose from and their Victorian-era ascribed meanings, I compared and contrasted. Adrienne was a Scorpio; I'd extracted that out of Donald, a Libra, long ago. So I, a Leo, could look up their general compatibility—fiery, fierce, forever passionate—in *Linda Goodman's Love Signs*, a fact-checking reference tool I'd used when I was editing an unauthorized biography of former *Dynasty* star Linda Evans and her composer-boyfriend, Yanni, and perpetually read her horoscope when I checked my own). Armed with this most fundamental bit of astrological knowledge, I first found our flowers and their meanings. Mine were gladiolus (temperance, trust) and larkspur (laughter); Adrienne's were narcissus (naturally) and chrysanthemum (abundance—*ref.:* her bust line). Our comparative gemstones proved equally disquieting: mine were ruby (clarity of heart) and sardonyx (marital happiness); Adrienne's were turquoise (prosperity, success) and lapis lazuli (power). I even checked the month we—Donald and I now; Donald and Adrienne then—planned on having the wedding. *Marry in April if you can, joy for maiden and for man*, was how the saying went.

One could, at this point, only hope.

But such small victories of investigation, such small insights into Adrienne's character were luxuries I would soon not be able to afford. My time, in the very near future, would have to be reserved for only the most important informational reconnaissance missions.

With such limited resources, with so little time, the Twins and I would have our work cut out for us.

18

But back to the dress.

Perhaps the biggest decision of all loomed large, and caused major physical and emotional distress. Unlike the reception menu, or the invitations, or the cake, it was certainly the one decision I could not make myself: how could I truly know how fat or hideous I looked in a particular dress without having someone there to tell me? Confiding in Gayle would be useless, I knew, but I confided in her anyway, which led her to offer to help me go dress shopping ("Get something with lots of texture and color!" she'd said). Which I declined, washing up instead yet again on the cold, rocky, unforgiving shores of Fran's store.

"I knew you'd be back," she snorted as she stubbed out her cigarette in the snow outside.

"What are those?" I asked, pointing at her feet. I'd never seen shoes anything quite like the ones she was wearing. Leather like a clog; zippered like a boot; with a transparent panel to showcase the toes.

"Not for you," she sniped. "You wouldn't know what to do with shoes like these."

Translation: *But Adrienne would, since she's so fabulously sophisticated and knows Dries Van Noten—and his mother— personally.*

My stomach dropped; I blinked away tears. Fran was particularly beastly at that moment—she hadn't slept well; hadn't had her coffee; had had only three out of her four morning cigarettes. But I couldn't afford to be sensitive. Following her past the customer-alert bell and to her throne at her desk with Olive at her feet, I stated my business in no uncertain terms:

"Help me," I said. "Help me find my wedding dress."

"I thought you'd never ask."

I assumed that meant yes.

"And thank God, too," she went on, needlessly, gratuitously. "You're going to need my help with that woman waiting in the wings."

"I know."

"Do you?" She sipped her coffee, stared me down. I recognized the look. She was about to pour salt in my wound; grind it in gleefully; set herself up as the only person who could save me. "Because competition doesn't get much worse than that."

"I know."

"I just want you to understand what you're up against."

She sat down, settled back in her chair, glanced at Olive and patted her head. (I marveled at how, with her dog, she was the picture of gentleness, while with people—me, for instance—she was anything but.) And then she asked me what kind of dress I thought I wanted.

I knew she couldn't have cared less what I wanted, since she would veto it immediately anyway. But I also knew I had to give her some answer, some direction, some sense of what I liked. After all, it was my wedding, and my dress. Wasn't it?

"Maybe Vera Wang . . . "

"Please," she said, with undisguised disgust, condescension. "Vera Wang is yesterday. Everybody wears Vera Wang. She's practically in malls, now."

Oh.

"What else?"

"Badgley Mischka," I said, "or however you pronounce his name." I'd seen several of his dresses advertised in high-end magazines' special wedding issues (*Town & Country; InStyle*), which was the extent of my knowledge.

"Their names."

"I'm sorry?"

"Their names. There's two of them: Mark and James." She thought a minute before dismissing *them*, too. "Look. You want something different. Something unusual. Something memorable."

"Well, not something as 'different' and 'unusual' and 'memorable' as your shoes," I said, feeling the old cynicism and sarcasm—the old me—surging back through my veins. "I mean, I still want to be able to tell that it's a dress."

She snorted again. "Don't worry. I know your limitations. What you want," she went on, "is something extremely chic."

"And attenuating," I added excitedly. Now we were getting somewhere.

"Something you're never going to find in Washington."

I sighed. "Which means?"

"Which means, you're taking us to New York to find your dress."

Although I hadn't intended on Gayle's going with us, when she got wind of the impending trip, over a quick Thai lunch that same day, she assumed she would be coming, too. Wide-eyed and salivating (she'd ordered her favorite noodle dish, and some fried fish balls that I never could stand the smell, let alone taste, of), she clasped her hands tightly as if the trip was the most exciting thing she could ever imagine participating in.

"Oh God! I cannot wait!"

"For what?" I thought maybe, on the off chance, she was talking about something else (lunch, for instance).

"To go to New York and shop for your dress, of course! I haven't been to New York in ages! And I've certainly never shopped in New York with a fashion expert the likes of Fran!"

I cleared my throat, then poked, picked at, and ultimately rejected, a fish ball. "I wasn't really planning on you coming."

She looked devastated. "But I must come!" she begged. "I simply must!" And then, as a last resort: "I can help!"

"Help what?"

"Well, I can hold things. Help you on and off with the dresses, and all the rest of it. Like some sort of medieval lady servant."

I was going to explain that the stores we would be going to (Barneys, Saks, Bergdorf's, and a few small boutiques on Madison Avenue and in SoHo) would have plenty of medieval-type lady servants to help me on and off with my clothes. But I realized all attempts to get Gayle to stay home would be futile. I drummed my fingers on the table; tried not to do the math:

Besides my round-trip weekend shuttle ticket, taxis, and my share of a now triple hotel room, I had planned, as a show of gratitude, on picking up Fran's not-so-incidental incidentals (cigarettes and triple Ketel One Vodka martinis). Would I now, to be fair, have to do the same when it came to Gayle?

Then there was the cost of the dress itself.

I shuddered to think what my credit card bill would look like.

I almost put my foot down and disinvited Gayle for real (the fact that I'd never officially invited her, and thus shouldn't have had to *disinvite* her, was already moot), but upon reflection, I knew it was a good idea to have her along, actually:

She would be a human buffer, protecting me from Fran.

19

Early the following Saturday morning, the first weekend in January, with overnight bags packed and shuttle tickets in hand, Gayle, Fran, and I met at the airport and boarded the eight-thirty flight to New York.

Since the plane was practically empty, Fran sat up front in her own double row of seats (her three, and the three across the aisle; she liked to stretch out); I sat, as usual, wherever destiny called (this time: 32A-B-C); and Gayle sat right behind me. It wasn't long before she was scratching at the upholstery and poking at me with her finger in between the seats.

I turned around, peered past her finger.

"Look!" she said, pointing to a huge pile of magazines on her lap that practically dwarfed her. "They're free!"

"Yes. I know."

"It's absolutely amazing! One could really sort of make a habit of this—getting so many free magazines—all for the price of a taxi ride to the airport and back."

I laughed, put my sunglasses on, popped half a Xanax. Was there anyone else in the world like Gayle? "You have to buy a shuttle ticket to get the free magazines. You can't just walk in off the street, pilfer the racks, and leave."

Silence for an instant, then the poking resumed. "But that rather defeats the purpose, does it not?"

I didn't bother to answer. Instead, I closed my eyes and, once the cabin door was shut and the plane taxied down the runway and took off, I settled into my rigid position for the duration of the flight.

When we were airborne, and the Xanax had taken effect, I moved slightly to open the window shade; looked into the clouds. I thought of Donald and how he was still sleeping when I'd left that morning, so early. Maybe it was my fear of death brought about by air travel (I quickly shut the shade: as we gained altitude, our near-vertical climbing angle into the clouds was too frightening to watch); or the realization that I couldn't remember the last time I'd told him I loved him, what with the pall of Adrienne's move hanging over us; or the sense of nostalgia that overcame me when I remembered that this was how he and I had met, almost two years ago exactly—flying together, on the shuttle—or the memory of his handsome, sleeping face, but I was suddenly overcome by the urge to call him, hear his voice, apologize for my bad behavior the past few months.

The plane leveled off, settled smoothly into its flight path; the attendants got busy with their infernal beverage cart; I detached the receiver of the phone on the back of the seat in front of me. Sliding my credit card through the slot (given what damage I was about to do when we landed, what difference could an outrageously expensive air-phone call make?), I dialed our home number. In seconds, through the static, I heard Donald pick up.

"Adrienne?"

My stomach dropped.

"Donald?"

"Adrienne?" he said again.

"No. It's Elise."

There was silence.

"Remember me?" I was crushed.

He laughed, or tried to anyway. "Oh! It's you! Adrienne just called me from her cell phone. We got disconnected and she said she was going to call right back. That's why I thought it was her."

"Well, it's not Adrienne. It's me. Sorry to disappoint you."

"I'm not disappointed."

Silence.

"How's the flight? Did you find a good seat?"

"It's fine." I wasn't in the mood for small talk or fear-of-death-induced niceties anymore. I rooted around in my bag and located, then swallowed, the other half of that Xanax with the bottle of water the flight attendant handed me. Papers were rattling on his end of the phone—or was that just static?

"Are you excited about the trip? Finding a dress? I'm sure Fran is going to help you find one that makes you look extremely tall. Not that I think you need to look tall, of course—I mean, any taller than you already are. . . ."

I was silent; my mind was racing. What was he doing talking to her so early in the morning? Especially on the one morning when I was on a plane leaving town? But since there was no way for me to know anything from twenty thousand feet up in the air, I decided to just end the call and endure the panic attack that was sure to follow.

"I have to hang up now," I said flatly.

"Wait," he said, his voice so low I could barely hear him now. "Was there something you wanted to tell me? A reason you called?"

Before I could think of the perfect comeback, there was a rush of static, then the connection was lost.

I turned and peered again back through the seat openings. There was Gayle, stuffing two fistfuls of (free) pretzel packets into her bag. I begged her to sit next to me immediately.

"What is it?" she asked, alarmed, in mid-packet, buckling herself into the aisle seat to my right.

"You're not going to believe this," I said. Then I told her about the phone call I'd just made and what Donald had said.

She chewed, swallowed, blinked wildly.

"Well?" I said.

"Well what?"

"What do you make of it?"

She started to reach for another packet of pretzels that she'd brought with her from her seat, but I took them away from her. "Answer me first!" I demanded.

She sat back, cleared her throat. "I'd say it happened exactly as he said it happened. Adrienne called him, they got disconnected, he was waiting for her to call back immediately."

Perverse as it may sound, that was not what I wanted to hear.

I wanted to hear a different explanation—something completely incriminating: Adrienne was calling him not from her cell phone, but from an air phone on the shuttle headed to Washington, where she and Donald would spend the weekend together while I was away; the minute I turned my back on him, he and Adrienne were in communication.

"Rubbish," Gayle pronounced, poking around my seat back for any uneaten packets of pretzels. "You're reading too much into things."

"Why are you always defending her?"

"I am not always defending her. I'm just trying to allay your supreme paranoia."

Just then, Fran appeared in the aisle. Judging from where a matchbook was inserted between pages, it looked as if she was more than halfway through one of those giant mass-market paperbacks that Anne had given me and I had given Fran. The midnight-blue and gold-foil cover, bent and cracked, was already showing the strain of Fran's abuse. "What are you two talking about?" she asked.

Gayle and I looked at each other, me trying to signal her not to tell Fran what I'd just told her about my phone call to Donald, but she didn't pick up on it. Instead, she sang like a canary.

"Oh, great," Fran said, rolling her eyes so vigorously that her entire head pivoted and her hair flopped from side to side, like a mop. "I'm wasting my one day off to help you find a dress for a wedding that might never even take place."

The pilot turned on the Fasten Seat Belt sign, announced we were beginning to descend. The verb seemed prescient; Fran returned to her seat, Gayle returned to hers, and I was left alone in mine to wallow in uncertainty and deep suspicion.

So absorbed was I in conspiracy theories (Donald had encouraged me to go to New York to shop, hadn't he? The incredible irony of my shopping for a wedding dress during their first, presumably, reconnective tryst must have made Adrienne scream with *Schadenfreude*) that I barely noticed our extremely bumpy landing.

Instead of calling Donald from my cell phone the minute we were on the ground, as I usually would to let him know I'd arrived safely, I decided to punish him for whatever he'd been doing with Adrienne earlier: I wouldn't call him, and I shut my phone off so he couldn't call me.

Taxiing from LaGuardia into midtown, we dropped our bags at the Regency Hotel, where Anne had arranged a room for us using her corporate discount. Then, after stopping briefly for coffee and a cigarette (Fran) and a fresh hot glazed Krispy Kreme doughnut (Gayle) at the first Starbucks we saw; and to take in Fifth Avenue in midtown on a quiet Saturday morning (me), we began our hunt.

First stop: Saks.

Nothing.

Second stop: Morgane Le Fay on Madison.

Nothing.

Third stop: Barneys.

Nothing.

Already exhausted, defeated, and hungry, we had a quick lunch at Fred's in the basement of Barneys before resuming our as yet fruitless search at Bergdorf Goodman sometime after three o'clock.

By now we knew the drill.

Fran would case the joint, deal with the salesperson, check the racks. If there was something even remotely interesting, she would have them bring the dress out in my size and order me to try it on; then she would force me to come out of the dressing room to model it. I would pad down the mock-runway stretch of cream-colored carpeting and pose—slouched, stiff, fingers splayed; left foot and toes, though unseen beneath the dress, curled under and dragging behind—and await their judgment.

Gayle loved everything.

Fran hated everything.

The salesperson didn't get a vote (Fran's rules).

I just wanted to go home and put an end to this charade. Fran was right. The wedding, at this point, would probably never take place.

"I've never seen such horrible dresses," she said, loudly, hoping to be overheard. "It's a good thing Recine isn't here today, or I would have told him what a loser he is for working here."

"Who's Recine?"

"One of the women's buyers. We get drunk every year after the shows."

I stared at her blankly.

"The fashion shows. In Milan. And Paris." Her eyes darted around the store, and I registered, for the first time, an almost undetectable trace of vulnerability in her: She'd never lived in New York. No matter how many times she'd been around the world, no matter how avant-garde the shoes she wore were, no matter how refined and forward-thinking her taste was, she would always be just a little bit out of her element here, just a little bit of an outsider.

"It's a good thing you might not need a dress now," she said, recovering her equilibrium quickly enough. "Because we might not find one."

"Thanks for your vote of confidence."

She slapped me on the back so hard that if I'd had a foreign object stuck in my throat, it would have been immediately dislodged and gone flying into somebody's hair. "Come on, Elise. I'm just kidding," she said, even though I knew she wondered if Donald and Adrienne were just a matter of time.

Suddenly, I heard Gayle squeal with delight. For a split second I thought she'd found the perfect dress.

"Look who's here!" she sighed.

I couldn't believe my ears, eyes. But there she was, Adrienne, looking unbelievably sexy in black spandex athletic pants, a black spandex long-sleeve T-shirt, and a perfect black leather car coat thrown over it. On her feet were the highest-tech sneakers I'd ever seen.

Great shock and surprise were expressed by all. Then, cheeks were kissed (Adrienne and Gayle; Adrienne and Fran); fingers were silently pointed (mine at Gayle); blame ascribed (Gayle, Gayle, Gayle).

"I was climbing—wall climbing—over at the gym at Chelsea Piers," she said, still breathless. "So I came straight from there."

"How did you know we were here?" I asked, certain she was going to nail Gayle.

"Donald had called me first thing this morning and he told me you were all coming up today to go dress shopping. I knew Bergdorf's had to be one of your stops. So I figured if I got lucky, I'd surprise you and say hello."

(Wait a minute: *Donald had called her? He'd said that she had called him.*)

"You can do more than that," Fran said. "You can help us find a dress."

"Nothing here?" she said, looking around. A translucent film of (athletic, fit, adventurous) sweat glazed her face, upper lip. I wished a giant mud slide would swallow me up, sweep me away, then deliver me to the nearest forensic pathologist who would find one person—and one person only—responsible for my demise.

"Nothing," Fran answered. "Nothing at Saks. Nothing at Barneys—"

"Did you try Morgane Le Fay?" Adrienne asked.

"Nothing at Morgane Le Fay. I don't know where else to look."

"What exactly is it you're looking for?"

Fran made a face, and Adrienne knew exactly what she meant.

"I know. The perfect, indescribable, nothing-else-quite-like-it-in-the-world kind of dress."

"Exactly," Fran said, sighing with relief. Finally. Someone who truly understood her vision.

Adrienne looked around, coolly assessed the severity of the situation, then dug around in her huge black nylon messenger-style gym bag. Peering into the bag over her shoulder I couldn't help noticing two small Ziploc baggies of chocolate miniatures—Krackels, Mr. Goodbars, Reese's cups—amidst the athletic gear. The hair on the back of my neck stood up. Had Donald given her that candy?

"Well, given the fact that this is an emergency," Adrienne said, "there's only one thing to do." She pulled out her cell phone, flipped it open, and commenced to speed-dial. "Let's call Dries. He owes me a favor."

Fran's jaw dropped.

Gayle blinked madly.

I died a thousand deaths. (For starters: *Who had international service on their cell phone besides Adrienne?*)

Listening to the beeping of her phone as it tried, then suc-ceeded in, connecting the call, Adrienne turned to us.

"Let's see, it's six hours ahead there now." She checked her Cartier Tank Française. "It's just after ten his time. I'm sure he's still at the *atelier*. He always works late." She turned away, smiled, spoke loudly into the phone.

"Dries!" And that was the last I understood, because the rest of the conversation took place in their common language: (what else?) French.

Fran, who didn't speak French ("I barely speak good English," she'd say), watched in awe. I jabbed Gayle in the ribs with my elbow. "Okay Miss Cambridge, start translating," I ordered.

She cleared her throat and began to paraphrase:

After some initial *prêt-à-porter* small talk (Adrienne had absolutely loved the samples he'd sent her from his forthcoming fall line, but they were actually *just a little big*—she'd lost some weight what with the emotional stress of the Francesco breakup and her impending move and new job), Adrienne got to the pur-pose of her call. She needed a favor. A very close friend (*Me? A close friend?*) was in a terrible fix. She was getting married in three months and needed something fabulous to wear.

A minute or so transpired; much (much too much) French was exchanged. Adrienne nodded, smiled, winked over at us. Then, after a few hundred *je t'aimes*, *d'accords*, and *bonsoirs*, she flipped her phone closed and rejoined us.

"He said he'd be happy to help. I told him we'd get your mea-surements, take a photo, and send it out DHL early next week. He promised to start on it as soon as possible."

The enormity of what was happening was just starting to hit me:

My fiancé's ex-fiancée was arranging for (controlling) the pro-curement of my wedding dress.

This dress, to be designed by Dries Van Noten himself, would cost a fortune.

I shook my head, waved my hands. *Stop the world, I want to get off.*

"Thank you so much, Adrienne, for calling him," I started, "but I couldn't *possibly* let him do this."

"Yes you can," Fran said.

"She can?" Gayle asked.

"She can," Adrienne finalized, then turned to me. "Dries and I are friends. Dear, dear friends. He'd do anything for me. This is a favor he's happy to do."

I shifted my weight.

Okay, so even if I was prepared to allow my fiancé's ex-fiancée to arrange for the procurement of my wedding dress, there was still the matter of the cost of a Dries Van Noten original.

"But what about . . . ?"

Adrienne waved her hand. "Don't worry about it. He would never expect to be paid for a gift to me. So, in turn, it is my gift to you. Consider it an early wedding present."

I swallowed a big gulp of air.

Did this mean she expected to be invited to the wedding now (assuming there actually was a wedding)?

"Or a heartfelt thank-you."

"For what?"

"For all your help with my move."

Speechless, boxed into a corner, and unable to get out of such a ridiculously shocking and completely unexpected situation, I nodded meekly.

"Thank you, Adrienne," I tried. "Thank you for . . ." I looked helplessly at Fran.

". . . for saving me from looking like an asswipe at my own wedding," she finished.

. . .

As we all left Bergdorf's together, filing onto the escalator one at a time, I purposely lagged behind. Watching Fran and Gayle on either side of Adrienne, still positively gushing over the stunt she'd pulled with Dries, and watching her perfect ass in those tight spandex pants (she'd taken off her leather coat right before she'd made the phone call) we descended floor by floor, as if into my own private hell.

Standing on the corner of Fifth Avenue and Fifty-seventh Street, buttoning our coats against the late afternoon January wind (the sun had disappeared; the temperature had plummeted; the cold grayness was an uncannily accurate mirror for my mood), I remained silent as the three of them discussed dinner plans. The consensus? That instead of getting all dressed up and going somewhere fabulous, we would get into comfortable clothes and go someplace where we could talk, get to know each other, eat like pigs.

"I know the perfect place," Adrienne said.

Of course she did.

"Kaplan's deli. At the Delmonico, right off Park, a block down from the Regency. They have the most unbelievable corned beef sandwiches."

Like she'd ever actually eaten one.

"Let me run home and change, and I'll meet you there in an hour."

Adrienne disappeared into a taxi; Gayle, Fran, and I headed over to our hotel, and after we'd checked in, we got our bags and headed up to the room. On the way there, Fran clapped me on the back again.

"Well, you're quiet."

"I'm in shock."

"You should be. Not everyone gets such an amazing windfall in the dress department."

I shoved the room key into the slot, pushed the door open, stared at Fran in disbelief. "How can you be so obtuse about this?"

She looked at me blankly.

"Dense. Clueless. Stupid," I said.

She hit me again. "I know what obtuse means."

I glared over at Gayle and pulled her into the circle of blame, too. "Don't either of you see what's going on? Adrienne, Donald's ex-fiancée, just picked out my wedding dress. The woman Donald was going to marry—and might still marry, at the rate I'm going—is involved in something as intimate and personal and private as what I'm going to wear to my own wedding. Not only that, she's infiltrating my group of friends—my best friends, the people I trust the most and hold dearest to me. She's seduced the two of you and clearly Donald's next. I mean, the second I'm out of town, he's on the phone with her, planning God knows what." I wanted to back up that allegation with the suspicious chocolates in her gym bag, but I was afraid it would damage my credibility instead of bolstering it.

Fran reached for a Merit Ultra Light, lit it. "Okay. I'll grant you the fact that the situation as you've just described it is certainly unconventional. But I'm not convinced anymore that Adrienne wants to cause trouble."

"Are you crazy? Of course she wants to cause trouble."

"Now, when I first met her, it was a different story. The minute she walked into my store I said to myself, 'This woman is up to no good.' " Fran flopped down onto the sofa, and rested an ashtray on her lap. "But now—I don't think so. I mean, Elise, she just called one of the most famous designers in the world on your behalf. Do you really think if she wanted to break you and Donald up that she would have just saved your ass the way she did? Making sure you're going to look unbelievably chic instead of letting you look like some off-the-rack Vera Wang loser?"

Gayle started nodding in vigorous agreement, but I shot her down with my sharpest look. I wasn't in the mood for two-against-one right now.

"Maybe it's more convoluted and more sinister than that," I said, sounding increasingly insane by the second. "Maybe she did that for the exact opposite reason: to make sure I look terrible at the wedding. Maybe she just asked him to make an incredibly ugly dress for me. Or one that won't fit. Or maybe, she'll tell him not to make anything so I'll have nothing to wear come April fifteenth."

Fran shook her head at me. "You're nuts. Look," she said, stubbing out her half-smoked cigarette. "I hate and distrust everyone. I'd be the first one to tell you if I suspected something. But I just don't think that's what's going on."

"So what *do* you think is going on?"

"You want to know what I think? Okay. This is what I think."

I sat down, braced myself.

"I don't think Adrienne wants Donald back. I don't think she wants to break the two of you up. I think Adrienne is lonely. I think she wants to be a part of Donald's life. And if that means befriending you — a woman who succeeded where she failed — in order to secure that place in Donald's life, then I think that's what she's determined to do."

I listened, then breathed a sigh of relief. Fran was probably right. Her reasoning certainly made sense. Maybe the situation wasn't as dire as I'd made it out to be. Adrienne's motives had been articulated, and the whole tableau was clarified — now all I had to do was figure out my role in all of it.

"So you think I should be friends with her?"

Fran considered the question carefully. I knew that despite her harshness and flipness, she was concerned for me; wanted the best for me; felt compelled to give me the soundest advice possible. Still, she couldn't help her sarcastic, eye-rolling tone. "Well, being afraid of her and letting her drive you crazy hasn't worked that well, has it?"

No, it hadn't.

For one thing, it had caused me to drop five hundred dollars on a sweater that I would probably never wear again because of its bad associations. For another, Adrienne had smelled my fear that day; had known I was intimidated by her, even in awe of her. Deep down, despite my misgivings and pride, I knew there was some truth to what Fran was saying. Still, I couldn't believe the trajectory of this conversation; this day. One minute I had two friends who were (seemingly) on my side; the next minute they were trying to convince me to surrender to the enemy.

"I'm not telling you to be her best friend or anything. But *you're* the one marrying *her* ex-fiancé, remember? You have the power here; you're the one winning. If you act like you don't care that she's around, like you don't care if she wants to get the occasional cup of coffee with Donald, that you're not threatened by her, it'll make you look like you're secure and self-confident. Even though, of course, we all know you're not."

Again, Gayle nodded in agreement.

"Now enough with this Jerry Springer bullshit," Fran said, unzipping her overnight bag and pulling a huge (brown) Eskandar sweater over her head. "I'm starving."

Later on, at dinner, with all of us in jeans (Adrienne in those perfectly tight Diesels) and our hair pulled up or back (hers expertly twisted in a tousled heap) and no makeup (could her skin, with an adorably faint dusting of freckles over the bridge of her nose, I saw now, possibly have been any clearer?), packed into a cramped table for four, I had to admit that maybe Fran was right. Maybe

Adrienne wasn't the malicious home-wrecking worst-nightmare beast I'd thought she was. Watching her inhale her corned beef sandwich and devour a huge black-and-white cookie for dessert; listening to her tell (somewhat) funny, charming (though completely narcissistic) stories about work ("So instead of getting fired, I ended up getting a huge raise!"); Francesco ("How many different ways was he going to threaten to kill himself if I didn't marry him? It was like *Harold and Maude!*") and mountain climbing ("So I stuck the pick into the ice and boom! I fell flat on my ass! Luckily, Tom Brokaw, who was making the climb with us, was there to catch me"), I felt she was one of us.

Or almost one of us.

Actually, she was nothing like us.

She would never be anything like us.

Still, whatever she was or wasn't, whatever her motives were or weren't, I knew I had to make a change in strategy.

Given the fact that she and Donald had been in touch behind my back that very morning, and would continue to be in touch once she moved to Washington (about the dog, if nothing else), I decided I'd better be careful not to inadvertently push them together by letting my paranoid jealousy show.

From now on, instead of fighting her, I would try to be friendly.

I would adopt or at least fake an attitude of strength; self-confidence; acceptance.

I would welcome her to our city with (semi) open arms.

And two weeks later, when she arrived in Washington, that's exactly what I did.

20

Instead of moving into that spacious, gracious apartment at the Kennedy-Warren, however, Adrienne moved into a fabulous Victorian on Morrison Street, about two miles further up Connecticut Avenue, right below Chevy Chase Circle (another friend of her father's, this one a professor at Georgetown going on sabbatical for a year, had bequeathed it to her at the eleventh hour).

I was shocked. This wasn't the plan!

Instead of being right around the corner where I could keep a close and constant eye on her if I needed to, Adrienne was now much further away. Upon reflection, though, I began to realize that there were distinct benefits to Adrienne's change of address: because she would be living in a house and not an apartment building, my surveillance could be far more precise. Her windows were street-level, her car would be parked in front of the house; with a quick glance, I could keep extraordinarily accurate tabs on her comings and goings.

Not to mention the fact that she could now indeed take the dog off our hands—have full custody of Lucy, in fact, we all agreed—until the wedding was over.

And so, committed to this new *glasnost*, this new attitude of live and let live, on the day of Adrienne's arrival I brought over two bags of (human) food from Dean & DeLuca and dropped them off at her house. Then I returned with two forty-pound bags of dog food and Donald to unload it.

Several days later, I helped her unpack her books (for starters: those infamous boxes of Russian novels that had spent so much time in Donald's closet) and shelve them, after which Donald helped rearrange furniture.

I also shared with her the names of doctors, dentists, cleaning people, car mechanics; told her where the best bakeries were (there weren't any, really, for humans, although there was an exceptional one for dogs in downtown Bethesda); where the best coffee shops were (there weren't any, really), while Donald took her on a tour of his gym.

The following week, I organized and picked up the tab for a welcome-to-Washington lunch with Fran and Gayle.

The week after that, we had Adrienne and Terrance (they were, it seemed, seeing each other) over for brunch, to officially celebrate her move.

Going through the motions of each of these helpful, friendly, neighborly, social occasions, I was surprised by how easy it was to pretend to embrace Adrienne instead of fighting her. Surprised by how easy it was to pretend not to be threatened. And surprised by how fulfilling it was. I'd given the Evil Twins their walking papers. I was being thoroughly modern. Incredibly French, if you will.

Donald, however, didn't seem to be faring quite as well. Whenever the three of us were together, I noticed more and more that he got a little green around the gills ("Oops! Sorry I dropped that"), tentative ("Can I just . . . ? Would you mind if I . . . ?"), overly agreeable ("Sure. Fine. Whatever. I don't care").

When the four of us got together—me and Donald, Adrienne and Terrance—he just got quiet. Pensive. Sometimes a little testy. The morning we had them to brunch, for instance, while Adrienne was telling us about the afternoon of Rollerblading through Rock Creek Park they'd had the day before, I caught him staring into his bagel (toasted onion with the merest *schmear* of low-fat cream cheese and Nova) so intently that I wondered if he expected his face to somehow be reflected in it.

When I nudged him with my elbow, he looked cross.

"What?" he said, staring at me.

I smiled tensely. "Nothing. I just—"

"You just what?"

"I just—you seemed distracted." I glanced over at Adrienne and Terrance, for support. Holding hands, they smiled politely, then tightened their grip.

They were no help. I sensed Donald bristling. Was it my comment, or their interwoven hands?

"I'm not distracted. I'm just eating," he said.

I nodded. "Okay. Sorry."

It was my comment.

Evidently trying to find a constructive way to pass the time while Donald and I hashed out our little problem, Terrance looked at Adrienne, swooned, then covered their already intertwined hands with his other hand. Crossing her legs, she gazed up at him, expertly managing to catch Donald's eye along the way.

Donald bristled again, pushed his plate away. He'd barely touched his bagel.

It was their hands.

Later, after they'd left, and we were in the kitchen cleaning up, it started.

"I feel fat," Donald said, running his hands over the usual suspects: hips, abdomen, stomach, chest. "I shouldn't have eaten that bagel."

"But you didn't eat that bagel. I don't think you even took one bite of it." I shut the water off, dried my hands on a dish towel, regarded him from across the room.

He was inconsolable.

"What is it?" I said.

He slumped into a chair at the table. "I'm just anxious."

"Anxious about what?"

"I feel like everything's out of control. My weight. The kids at school. Our wedding."

"What about our wedding?" I wondered, suddenly, if this was the moment he was going to tell me he didn't want to get married after all.

"I keep thinking we're forgetting something. You're sure all the deposits are in?"

I nodded slowly. I had no idea where this was coming from, or where it was going. "Donald—is there something else?" I asked. But he kept his eyes down, wouldn't look at me.

"Everything's just annoying me lately. For instance, Ron, this seventh-grade teacher, saw me getting out of my car the other morning and made fun of me all day."

"What did he say?"

"He said, 'I see you took the family station wagon today.' "

I waited; asked if there was more. There wasn't.

"He's just jealous," I said.

"Of what?"

"Your car."

"I don't think so."

"Of course he's jealous of your car. I mean, you're a teacher and you drive a BMW 740, remember?"

"But he drives a Saab Turbo convertible."

I tried again. "Well, is he short?"

"No, not particularly. He's shorter than me, of course, but he's at least six feet. He's one of the varsity basketball coaches."

I was at a loss. I had no idea why this guy had made fun of Donald. Plus, I was losing my patience, distracted because I was supposed to have made a big dent over the weekend in *The Misunderstood Calorie: Why Fat Doesn't Make You Fat*. As usual, I was way behind. I eyed the pile of pages across the room on the counter next to all the bagels and lox and cream cheese waiting to be put away. Fat didn't make you fat. Would the absurdity never end?

"Maybe it was something about the way I was dressed. Or the way I was physically getting out of the car. Do I look funny when I get out of the car?" He thought a minute, exhaled, shook his head. "And Terrance is bugging me a lot, too, lately."

Aha.

"He's always cornering me in the hallway, or in the teacher's lounge, telling me about Adrienne: what they did, where they went; asking me about what I think it means when she said this or did that. As if I know. As if I have a blueprint of what goes on in her head."

As if he'd give it up and hand it over to Terrance if he did.

"It's driving me crazy."

I'll bet it was.

"They're seeing a lot of each other?" I asked.

"Once, twice a week, he says."

"You think it'll get serious?"

He rolled his eyes, looked at me like I should know better. "Honey! Come on!" He laughed too loudly, humorlessly. "I mean, he's a little out of his league!"

A *little?* I called that shot a long time ago.

"He doesn't know whether he's coming or going!" Donald laughed again. "I don't think he knows what he's gotten himself into. I mean, she's . . . she'll . . ." He shook his head: apparently he knew all too well what Terrance was in for. "A month from now, two months from now, she'll have him wound so tightly around her little finger he won't even remember his own name." He sat back in his chair, sighed, looked sad. "Plus—" he started.

"Plus what?"

"Plus, I miss Lucy. I'm not used to not having her around."

I sat down at the table with him, surprised at how rational, how unflappable the New Me was.

The Old Me, of course, would have gone crazy by now, mad with suspicion and paranoia.

But not the New Me.

Adrienne had moved here, out of the blue, three months before our wedding, was living less than two miles away from us, had co-opted both my best friends and interfered with the selection of my wedding dress, was dating one of Donald's best friends (which was clearly starting to bother him), was everything I was not, with her rock climbing, love of aviation and adventure, and perfect perfect ass. . . .

But so what? I'd banished the Evil Twins weeks ago, faced my nemesis and survived. I felt strong. Free. Invincible.

Until, that is, the moment when the whole thing backfired and Adrienne stabbed me in the back.

21

Adrienne's betrayal was swift, unexpected.

The three of us—she, Donald, and I, Terrance was out of town—had gone to dinner together at Palena, the restaurant Donald had taken me to the night he proposed. We'd ordered a bottle of wine; had just received our first course. When all of a sudden, Adrienne turned to Donald, nudged his arm with her elbow and said:

"So I hear you're going to get liposucked before the wedding."

He dropped his fork.

Then I dropped mine.

"Where did you hear that?" He turned beet red; glared at me, the only person in the world he'd told.

She nudged again. "I have my sources."

He looked at me again, and I blanched guiltily. "Yes, I guess you do," he said.

I was mortified. I'd almost completely forgotten that I'd divulged such a confidential bit of information to Adrienne, but in my haste to become her friend, I'd let this slip out. I'd betrayed Donald's privacy.

Of course, the minute I'd done it, I regretted it.

Please, I'd begged. *Please don't tell Donald I told you. He'd die if he found out anyone else knew.*

She'd squeezed my arm, then, the way new best friends do:

Don't worry, squeeze squeeze. *You can trust me.*

How could I have been so stupid?

Why hadn't I seen that she was setting me up? That she was just waiting for me to speak out of turn?

I leaned across the table, tried to take Donald's hand—a gesture of sincere contrition—but he wouldn't let me. Instead, he smiled broadly.

"Well, okay. I admit it. I was going to have liposuction before the wedding. But I changed my mind."

"You did? When?" I asked, but he barely acknowledged me; continued to talk directly to Adrienne.

"A few weeks ago I just realized I could probably achieve the results I want with diet and exercise, instead of going through such a grotesque surgical procedure."

Which is exactly why he'd wanted to have liposuction in the first place: because he felt that diet and exercise *weren't* giving him the results he wanted.

"And what results are those, exactly?" Adrienne queried.

"To get rid of this," he said, grabbing at nonexistent pockets of flesh above and toward the back of his hips, right near the kidneys. "My love handles."

Adrienne laughed. "But you don't have love handles."

"Yes I do," he insisted. "I've always had love handles."

"No you haven't," she offered. "You didn't have them when we were together, and you don't have them now."

She looked at me for the first time since she'd spilled the beans, and I could see the old gleam in her eyes. She'd extracted a precious little nugget of information out of me about Donald; she'd used it to bust me; now she was gloating in the power she held to make him feel better. All of this to get closer to him and terminate our budding friendship, if that's even what it was. I felt idiotically naive, and also inexplicably sad: as if I'd lost a new friend whom I'd really really liked but who had clearly never really liked me.

Adrienne?

A *friend*?

Whom I *really really liked*?

Was I completely crazy?

"I didn't have love handles when we were together?" Donald continued. Despite himself, her reassurance was working.

"No. You didn't."

"And you don't now," I threw in, hoping he would see that I, too, had his best interests at heart. But he ignored me, waited for Adrienne to continue plying him with compliments.

"You look amazing," she said for what seemed like the thousandth time. "I told you that the minute I saw you back in November. You look better than I ever remember you looking."

His face grew serious. She was gazing at him with her big brown eyes, pushing his buttons expertly. "How so exactly?" he urged. "I mean, how exactly do I look better?"

She considered the question. "Fitter. Thinner. You know, like I said, you look fantastic." She reached over and touched his wrist with her pinkie finger, then combed her fingers through her hair.

His hands then ran feverishly over his abdominal region, along and around his belt to the kidney area in question. Suddenly, they stopped their incessant search for excess flesh, and he sat back, and breathed out slowly.

"I know you always thought I was crazy about my weight, but I was a fat kid. And because of that I'll always think I'm fat. No matter how much weight I lose; no matter how many people tell me I'm not."

Adrienne's eyes glazed over with tears. Now she took his hand, gave it a little squeeze. Then her eyes shot over to me, glittering with silent victory. Even if I could have thought of something to say, I wouldn't have dared to speak. She'd made it known that I'd done enough damage already.

Our entrées arrived; the meal proceeded with almost undetectable discomfort; but coffee and dessert were declined by all (most vociferously, of course, by Donald). Clearly, it was time to part company.

Once out on the street, Adrienne went to the right to get her car and head up Connecticut; we went to the left to walk the few blocks home down Connecticut in complete and utter silence.

But when he put the key in the door and stormed through the house toward the kitchen, he let me have it.

"I can't believe you did that! I can't believe you told her something I considered extremely personal and private, and which you knew was extremely personal and private."

I nodded miserably. "I know. I know. And I'm so, so sorry."

"You're *sorry?*" he said. "That was one of the most embarrassing moments of my life. Adrienne knowing about the liposuction. *Anyone* knowing about the liposuction. You were the only person in the world I felt close enough to tell, the only person in the world I trusted enough to tell, and you betrayed that trust. I should be able to rely on you to protect me, to not compromise me in any way, to stand by me and be completely and absolutely loyal. I deserve at least that much. I mean, Jesus, Elise! *We're getting married in three months!*"

I nodded again and again.

"What were you thinking?" he asked, confounded, mystified. "How could you have done that?"

"I don't know," I said. And truly, I didn't. "It was an accident."

Dr. Frond, however, would have dismissed my explanation instantly. "Saying 'I have done something by accident' is just a self-protective psychological euphemism for saying 'I did it on purpose,' " she would have pronounced in her mysterious, unidentifiable Eastern European accent. "No one wants to believe they are capable of immoral, unethical behavior; of indiscretion, deceit, betrayal. No one wants to believe they are capable of hurting people they love. And so they blame it on 'an accident.' Perhaps you are not acting consciously when you commit these breaches of trust, but your psyche is."

Is that what had happened?

Had I betrayed Donald "accidentally on purpose" because I was angry at him for wanting to have a relationship with Adrienne?

Had I so wanted Adrienne to like me that I gave her something I should never have given her? Something so hilarious and ridiculous about Donald that it would instantly bring us together, make us bond at his expense? Had I believed that by bonding with Adrienne, I could neutralize her? Disarm her? Stop her from coming between Donald and me, if that's what she had come to Washington to do?

Was I still so insecure, so mistrustful, so full of Gloom and Doom about Donald and the future of our union, that I had to sabotage our relationship? End it before it ended me?

Donald sighed deeply. I didn't blame him. I felt the same way. I was hurt and confused about the pain I had caused him. But, I realized, I was hurt and confused about the pain Adrienne had caused me.

Our friendship, however brief it was, however false it may have been, was over. She had used me. My fleeting fantasy of having a sophisticated, modern, and mature relationship with Donald's ex-fiancée was finished. I had failed in my mission to win her over, to outsmart her. What Fran had said that time was true: I wasn't tough enough to handle the game I was playing. I had been in over my head the whole time.

In the hours and days that followed, I ate fistfuls of chocolate miniatures; took long drives through the streets of our neighborhood, thinking about what I'd done, how stupid I'd been. There was a perceptible, obvious chasm between Donald and me now. A line had been crossed—by me—and I was afraid that I'd done irreparable damage to him and to our relationship:

He didn't trust me; he never would; our life together as we'd known it was truly over. For real this time.

But Donald being Donald—trusting, loving, forgiving—in a week he seemed willing to let it go. The following Sunday morning, as we had a late breakfast together in the kitchen he not only absolved me of guilt, shame, and malice aforethought and intent, but he dismissed the incident unilaterally, attributing my uncharacteristic behavior to pre-wedding insecurity.

Insecurity?

I hated to look a gift horse in the mouth, but I couldn't help feeling that the word needed a bit of clarification.

"Insecurity," he repeated, matter-of-factly. "About Adrienne."

I nodded slowly, dubiously. I didn't like the sound of this.

"In retrospect, I guess I can see why she made you so crazy."

"And why was that?"

"Well, I mean, isn't it obvious?" He waited for me to answer, but I didn't. I was dying to hear what he would say next; how he would hang himself. "You thought if you befriended her she wouldn't hurt you. She's a force."

Pause.

"She's a force to be reckoned with."

Pause.

"A force to be dealt with."

Pause.

"A force to be resisted."

Oops.

"*Resisted?* As in temptation-wise?"

"Yes. She's an extremely charismatic person. And she can be very seductive when she wants to be. A woman as beautiful as Adrienne knows she can get anything she wants."

I'd just about had enough.

"Quit pussyfooting around, Donald," I finally exploded. "Just say what you mean."

"I am saying what I mean. For the past few months you've been obsessing about her, about her and me. All I'm saying is that I understand why she made you crazy."

"This isn't about me, Donald. This is about you. What you're really trying to say is that Adrienne is making *you* crazy. Because

Adrienne is incredibly alluring. Because she's a temptress. You're having a hard time resisting her charms and this is your way of telling me that you're conflicted, that we're in trouble."

And with that final declaration I grabbed my bag, my car keys, my phone, and fled the house.

22

I had no idea where I was going when I slammed the door behind me and jumped in my car, but I did know this much:

I was melting down.

Stopping first at the coffeehouse of Politics and Prose for a giant "Changes in Latte-Tude" (how portentously appropriate now), I then got back in the car and tore out of the parking lot, unsure of what to do next. But the Evil Twins weren't unsure. They knew exactly what I would do:

I would proceed directly to Adrienne's house for a quick middle-of-the-day Sunday drive-by.

Seconds later, there I was, slumping down in the driver's seat behind the wheel; lowering the visor and angling it against the window to obscure half of my face; whizzing past her house. Sweating, my heart beating wildly, I got to the end of her block and tried to figure out what I'd seen:

Nothing.

Perhaps I'd driven by too quickly.

I took a right, another right, then another right, making a little box and ending up right where I'd started: driving down her street, whizzing past her house, staring out the window. This time, though, I slowed down just enough to take in the scene, process it once I'd passed:

Again, nothing.

No newspapers on the lawn or steps. No lights on (it was just after noon, and fairly sunny). Her car out front. Nothing of any interest whatsoever.

Though the Evil Twins were not convinced (they were certain all was not as innocent as it seemed at 2921 Morrison Street), I breathed a short sigh of relief: at least I knew where she was and where Donald wasn't. I then made a right, then another right, then a left this time onto Connecticut and headed back toward home. Only I didn't stop when I got to our street. Instead, I kept going, veered left, got onto Rock Creek Parkway, and headed for Georgetown.

Luckily, Gayle's car (an ancient maroon Volvo wagon) was there when I pulled up in front of her town house. I screeched to a halt; ran up the front stairs; knocked loudly. She came to the door looking somewhat ridiculous in a stiff short-sleeved wildly patterned men's button-down shirt. I couldn't help staring at her sinewy slender arms as I walked into the foyer.

"What?" she said, squirming under the glare of my disapproving gaze.

"Nothing," I said, trying to suppress my desire to criticize, but I couldn't. "You look like Linda Hunt in that shirt."

She stopped short. "What do you mean?"

"I mean, you look like Linda Hunt, in *The Year of Living Dangerously.*"

"When she played that little man, the one who jumps out of the window at the end?"

I nodded.

She covered her mouth with her hand in shame. "What must I do?" she whispered.

"Get rid of that shirt."

She peered down at herself, touched the fabric. "But I love this shirt. Look," she said, moving closer to me, as if to show me one of nature's great miracles. "It's so visually complex."

"I don't care. Get rid of it."

"Yes, I see," she said sadly. "Tomorrow."

"No. Today. Please."

You'd think I would have been unable to concentrate on anything but my crisis at hand—that morning's fight with Donald about Adrienne—especially on something as meaningless as Gayle's stupid shirt. But somehow, that's all I could concentrate on at that moment. For had I focused on what was really going on—that I was, single-handedly and for seemingly no reason, destroying my relationship with Donald and risking our upcoming nuptials—I probably would have fallen face down on my bed and not been able to get up.

Which is exactly what I did when I followed Gayle upstairs to her dizzyingly "visually complex" bedroom, filled with raw silk curtains, deeply colored lampshades, patterned throws and rugs.

Still wearing the ridiculous shirt, she rushed over to me, bent down to see my face. "What is it?" she asked, her voice full of concern. "What is wrong with you?"

I moaned; turned my head away; felt myself starting to drool onto a beaded pillow. "My life," I mumbled. "My life is a mess."

She asked why; I explained.

Her brow became deeply furrowed. "Why are you doing this?" she asked.

"Doing what?"

"Ruining your life?"

She sat down on the edge of the bed, nudged me gently on the arm to get my attention. "Remember what I told you that morning in the car, on our way to pick Adrienne up at the airport?"

I rolled onto my back; stared at the antique reproduction *Casablanca*-inspired ceiling fan.

She nudged again. "Remember I told you that this whole situation was a test? A test of faith? Of trust? Of your love for Donald and his love for you?"

It seemed like years had passed since we'd had that conversation. I smoothed my palms over the sheets and comforter cover, and closed my eyes. I felt old suddenly. Old and very, very tired.

"Yes," I finally answered. "So?"

"*So?*" She nudged again, harder this time. "So, you're failing. You're failing the test I told you you absolutely could not fail."

I propped up two oversized velvet pillows, sat with my back

against them. Speechless, I stared at Gayle. She was right. We were both failing that test, Donald and me.

Miserably. Epically. With flying colors.

"I don't know what to do," I said. "How to reverse it. How to stop this . . . downward spiral. I'm so paranoid I even drove by Adrienne's house on the way here. I don't trust him, and now he doesn't trust me. I betrayed him, and now I'm afraid he will finally betray me: he'll go back to her like I've always suspected he would."

"Look, listen," she started, her voice stern, "you have no reason in the world to think that. Donald has said nothing, done nothing to lead you to believe he is going to leave you for Adrienne. This is all simply a figment of your overactive imagination."

She blinked; I blinked; we said nothing.

"Now get up and let's go."

I sat up, took note. "Go where?"

"Do you not follow?"

I shook my head; I didn't.

"You and I are going to drive by Adrienne's house again, of course. And this time, when you find nothing and see that there's absolutely no reason for you to be acting so crazily, you will, once and for all, finally be cured of these ridiculous thoughts."

First, we drove by our house, Donald's and mine. And when we did, his car was gone.

"He's not here," I said to Gayle.

"Yes I can see that."

I felt full of dread. "Maybe he's with her."

"Stop it!"

"No really. Maybe after our fight, he got so fed up with me and my lunacy that he just got in the car and drove straight over to her house. Maybe he's been there all this time. Since right after I drove by and went to your house."

"You are mad," Gayle pronounced. I hoped and prayed she was right.

I was speeding up Connecticut now, up past the small scruffy patch of urban campus that was the University of the District of Columbia at Van Ness; up past Politics and Prose again; up past the sparse clusters of neighborhood dry cleaners and restaurants and drugstores and into Chevy Chase. I swerved, changed lanes at will. As we approached the Safeway, I screeched over two lanes from the left-most one and took a sharp right onto Morrison Street.

I immediately slowed down and, like an athlete, got into position: slouch, slump, visor down, sunglasses on. Then on the final approach to her house, I picked up speed, whizzing by as quickly as I could. Only this time, when I stopped at the end of the block to process the scene, my stomach dropped. Donald's car was there, out in front of her house, parked just ahead of hers. I looked in the rearview mirror just to make sure and saw it again.

I turned to Gayle, clung to her arm. "He's there," I said, my voice cracking. "He's in there, with her."

Gayle wrung her hands guiltily. She had been the one, she was thinking, to cause this debacle.

I backed the car up a few feet and parked under a huge oak tree, about six houses down from Adrienne's. Safely out of sight, I could still see Donald's car in both my rearview and left-side mirrors (all those years of watching reruns of *Columbo, The Rockford Files, Mannix,* had paid off: I knew how to tail a perp like the best of them).

I looked at Gayle, begged for advice. "So, should I sit here until he leaves? Then confront him?"

"Look, listen," she started. "I have no idea . . . "

But I wasn't paying attention anyway. "Or should I just go in there? Walk up the stairs, knock on the door, catch them red-handed, in the act."

Gayle was wringing her hands so violently I was afraid she might actually do some damage to her skin and flesh.

"I'm going to drive by again, to see if there's anything else I can see."

"Oh God!" Gayle breathed, but before she could finish her thought, I had already pulled out and headed off down the street to start making my box. Seconds later, whizzing past Adrienne's house for the second time, I stopped again, trying to make sense of what I'd seen.

"I think I saw him. Inside. Those front windows are the living room. I think he was in there."

"Was he with her?"

"I don't know. I think I saw someone else."

"Are you sure?"

"No I'm not sure." I craned my neck to look out through the back of the car, but I couldn't see anything. "I mean, I think I saw two people in there. But the other one didn't look like Adrienne."

"Who did it look like?"

"I don't know. I think it looked like Donald."

"You mean, Donald and another person who looked like Donald?"

I wasn't certain; didn't answer.

"Does Donald have a twin?" she asked.

I turned to her. "Don't you think I would have told you if he had a twin?"

"Well, yes, I suppose you would have. I was just trying to be helpful."

"Well, you're not."

"Well, I'm sorry."

"Well, don't pout."

"I'm not pouting. I'm just trying to—"

"Look, I'm sorry I snapped, but surveillance is a high-pressure high-stakes game, Gayle. It's an inexact science. Your eyes play tricks on you. Vision, under extreme stress like this, is highly subjective; sometimes deceiving." I had no idea what I was saying, jabbering on like that, like Bill Kurtis on *Investigative Reports* or *American Justice*. But I was so overwrought that nothing made sense: I wasn't sure who, if anyone, was in Adrienne's living room, the living room I'd helped set up by shelving all those stupid books of hers. Readjusting my rearview and side mirrors didn't help. I could only see Donald's car, not Adrienne's house.

There was only one solution.

"We're going to have to drive by again," I pronounced.

I careened yet again around the block; whizzed by the house. Afterwards, I parked under the same big oak tree; shut the car off.

"Did you get a better look?" she asked.

I closed my eyes, tried to process the scene I'd just seen. "No. I did not." In fact, this time, I didn't think I saw anyone at all. Which made me even more curious. Had they (Donald and Adrienne, presumably) indeed been in the living room together (standing; talking; planning for their future)? And had they just moved into a different part of the house (upstairs); into a different room (bedroom)? Just as I was considering yet another drive-by, Gayle poked me in the arm.

"Start the car," she ordered. "We're leaving."

I turned to her. "*Excuse* me?"

"You heard me. I said start the car. We're leaving right now."

"We most certainly are not leaving. We're sitting here until Donald comes out—if he ever comes out. And then I'm going to confront him. Get it all out into the open."

"Get *what* out into the open?"

I stared at her, completely stupefied. "Their affair, of course!"

"That is the most farfetched unsubstantiated accusation I have ever heard in my whole life. You have absolutely no proof that Adrienne is after Donald. And you have absolutely no proof that Donald is after Adrienne."

"Oh yes I do."

"What do you have?" she said, and poked again. "Tell me every last bit of evidence you have that Donald and Adrienne are conspiring against you; that they're seeing each other romantically." Then she sat back against the car door, satisfied that she'd show me, finally, that I had nothing.

"Okay, for starters," I started, "there was the night she came to dinner and they flirted shamelessly all night long."

"I was there," Gayle countered, "and they did no such thing."

"Yes they did. You were just too busy wolfing down your poached pears and choking on them to notice."

"I didn't choke on the pear because I was eating too much or too quickly. I choked because I simply swallowed what I was eating the wrong way."

That's right. Adrienne's Einstein's brain story had gotten in the way.

"There was the time I called Donald from the shuttle to New York and he thought I was Adrienne," I continued. "And then how he sounded weird and nervous and solicitous right afterwards."

"Well of course he sounded weird and nervous and solicitous—he'd just answered the phone thinking it was Adrienne and he knew you'd be furious. Which you were."

"Which I was. And which I had a right to be."

"What else?"

"The whole wedding dress fiasco. How Adrienne interfered. Which was her way of controlling me; her way of living vicariously through me, since she wishes *she* were the one marrying Donald."

"What else?"

"How bothered he's been about Terrance and Adrienne dating—having to hear about it every day at school—how jealous it's obviously making him, his ex-fiancée dating his close friend." I paused a minute, came up for air. "Not to mention the fight we had today—him telling me that Adrienne is a force to be resisted. That she can be very seductive. Not to mention *right now, this very minute.* He's in her house, Gayle, as we speak, doing God knows what."

"My point exactly!" she said. "You don't know what he's doing in there. Maybe he's changing a light bulb. Fixing her sink. Hanging a picture. Maybe she called him and begged him to come over and help her because there was a huge bug in her bathtub and she was afraid to kill it herself. Maybe she called him because she was starving, hadn't eaten a decent meal in days, and begged him to bring over some provisions."

"Or, *maybe,* she begged him to come over because she's incredibly lonely and still in love with him and she thought she'd make her move now while there was still plenty of time to break us up before the wedding."

I could tell Gayle was almost at the end of her rope: her eyes darted around the car as if she were literally looking for a way out, for a way to leave me alone with my madness. But she was far too loyal a friend to abandon me in my hour of need.

And also, far too hungry. It was way past lunchtime, after all, and I knew she thought there might be a way to salvage the disastrous day by tucking into a good meal.

"Listen, perhaps we could—"

"No," I said, stopping her dead in her tracks. "We're not having lunch. I'm not hungry. And the last thing I feel like doing is watching you stuff yourself at a time like this."

She wiped at the dust on the dashboard. "Well. I see." Her

feelings were hurt. And why wouldn't they be? Here she was, trying to make a bad situation better. The least I could do was feed her.

I checked the rearview and side mirrors: no change in the status of Donald's car. "All right," I said, "I'll make a deal with you. We'll stay here until Donald leaves—however long that is—and afterwards, we'll eat."

"Okay," she said. "That's sounds like a good deal."

"It is."

"But when do you think that might be?"

"When what might be?"

"The payoff, as it were. When we might eat?"

Just as I was about to read her the riot act, something caught my eye in the left-side mirror:

Donald walking to his car.

With Adrienne.

I grabbed the steering wheel, unsure of what to do. Then I grabbed Gayle.

"Down!" I yelled, as if we were in a foxhole. "Get down!"

Slumped low in my seat, I somehow managed to keep a constant eye on the mirror.

Donald and Adrienne talked for a few minutes next to the car, expressionless, emotionless, a (fairly) safe distance apart.

She nodded, then he nodded, as if they'd just arranged something, and he stepped away.

She smiled, then patted him on the arm, then reached up and kissed him on the cheek.

He leaned over, awkwardly, and kissed her on the cheek.

Then he unlocked his door, slid in, started the engine, and pulled out slowly into the street and toward us.

Knowing there was nowhere to hide, I prayed he would not notice my car (let alone, me and Gayle in it). A second or two clicked by. His 740 passed right by my (thankfully ubiquitous) black Jetta, then made a right at the end of the street. I knew he was going to make a half-box, back out onto Connecticut, and probably go home.

I started the ignition.

"Are we going to have lunch now?" Gayle asked. I shot her another scathing look and, knowing what was good for her, she immediately changed the subject. "Shall we follow him? Or do you think he's just going home?"

I wasn't sure. Keeping a safe distance, I pulled out into the street, made a right and another right, and saw Donald's car heading south on Connecticut. Figuring he was indeed headed home, and figuring, too, that there was nowhere more incriminating that he could possibly be headed than where he'd just come from, I decided I would give up the search. For now. I crossed Connecticut and drove straight down Livingston Street to Reno Road and stopped at the light, which had just turned red.

My heart was pounding; my hands shaking. I hadn't realized what a shock to the system it was to see Donald and Adrienne together like that, in secret; how devastating it was to have my worst suspicions confirmed. Seeing them there in the street, by his car, moving as if in slow motion, as if in some underwater pantomime; not knowing what was going to happen next (*Would they embrace? Kiss? Would she get into the car? Would they drive off together, never to be heard from again?*), I felt the aftermath of a traumatic event: fear and shock subsiding into numbness.

I turned to look at Gayle and, despite the incredible tension of the moment, I could have died laughing. She was still in the emergency slump position, not having moved a muscle since I'd yelled at her to get down. Her eyes were big and round; her skin ashen. She wasn't even blinking.

"God. That was terrifying. Absolutely terrifying. What would we have done if they'd seen us?"

"I don't know."

"It was my first time getting away in a getaway car, you know. And hopefully it will be my last."

I knew it would not be mine, though.

"You know how I can barely read my international espionage books without my hands shaking. The stress is too much for me."

I did know. Her longtime fascination with the escapades of Kim Philby, the British double agent, was purely an armchair obsession, not something she wanted to experience firsthand. Which made me even more appreciative suddenly of her sticking by me, crouching in fear, just now, in the car. I knew I'd have to find a way to make it up to her when this was all over.

The light changed, and I inched forward, continuing to drive as if on automatic pilot. Before I knew what I had done, I found myself pulling into the back parking garage of Krupin's deli, just off Wisconsin Avenue.

Gayle rallied, practically hugged me. It was one of her favorite restaurants, and one of Donald's favorites, too, since it was the closest thing in Washington to a New York diner.

"A good hot meal will do us both good," she said, as we walked toward the elevator. "I think I'll get the brisket sandwich. Or the stuffed cabbage. Or maybe a matzo ball soup with the brisket sandwich and a side order of stuffed cabbage. . . ."

I stopped listening. Her voice was like the fading call of a nearby bird, slowly disappearing into white noise. And as it did, I couldn't help reliving, over and over again, those shocking moments in front of Adrienne's house. Remembering the horrifying scenes in *The Portrait of a Lady* in which Isabel Archer continually comes upon her husband with the worldly, smiling Madame Merle, I couldn't help but feel devastated: even Donald, the most honest, true, loyal man I'd ever known and had ever hoped to know, couldn't be trusted.

I followed Gayle to the hostess stand, where we were handed

menus and waved forward to our table. So lost in thought was I about the day's terrifically depressing events that I barely noticed when Gayle turned around, full circle, and said, rather loudly: "He's here!"

"Who?" I asked.

"Donald! Over on the right! In a booth!"

I felt my adrenal glands go into overtime for the second time that day. I didn't know how much more of this extreme shock I could take. Looking across the restaurant, I saw what Gayle had seen: Donald, sitting quietly in a turquoise pleather booth, his head of wavy hair lowered. He was drowning his sorrows in a bowl of chicken soup and a Reuben sandwich.

A child of divorce, Donald always had been completely susceptible to comfort food.

There were two options, and only seconds to decide between them: Either we would sneak past Donald to our table and not acknowledge his presence, or we would go up to his table and pretend we hadn't just spent the last hour spying on him and Adrienne (leaving the restaurant altogether without eating wasn't an option, I knew, with Gayle in tow) —

Donald was standing up suddenly, beside the booth, waving frantically. Oddly enough, he seemed incredibly happy to see us.

"I'm so glad to see you both," he said, smiling warmly (sheepishly?) at me as Gayle and I stood there, holding our plastic menus. "What are you doing here?"

Gayle looked like she was ready to burst at the seams, barely able to keep herself from telling Donald everything that had happened, so I forced myself to answer his question:

"We were just," I said tauntingly, "driving by. Gayle was hungry."

Donald tried to catch my eye, but I avoided looking straight at him. I couldn't bear to face him right now, knowing what I knew.

"Big surprise," he said, trying to engage me in a private joke about Gayle's incessant appetite, but I just eyed him coldly.

Gayle, ignoring any psychological subtleties, drove the point home. "Yes, I'm famished."

A second or two lapsed; Donald looked at each of us, then at the table. "Come on. Sit down. Join me."

Before I could protest, invent an excuse, Gayle slid into the booth. Reluctantly, I slid in after her.

"What a horrible day it's been," Donald said, poking at his matzo ball with his spoon. His sandwich, was, as yet, untouched.

"Oh God, for us too!" Gayle blurted.

Donald looked up from his bowl of soup. "Really? Why?"

She looked like she was ready to spill the beans again, so I stepped in.

"Traffic," I said.

"Really?" Donald looked puzzled "Where?"

"Everywhere."

On Morrison Street, mainly.

Where there was an unusual pileup of parked vehicles.

Due to apparent rubbernecking, staking-out, perp-searching.

Gayle looked longingly for the waiter. I glanced at the back flap of my menu (lox and eggs; pastrami and eggs; salami and eggs; tongue on rye) and wanted to barf.

"Why was it so horrible for you?" I asked Donald, remembering suddenly that he was the one who had brought it up.

He continued to play with his food. "Well, first, you and I get into that stupid fight. And that depressed me. And then I come here and order all this food, which I shouldn't eat." He smiled at me, then reached out for my hand, but I moved it before he could touch me. Which seemed to instantly concern him: he had no idea why I was being so cold.

The waiter arrived; took Gayle's order (soup; brisket sandwich on challah bread; extra coleslaw; one stuffed cabbage roll; cream soda); and mine (Diet Coke). I turned to look at Donald, decided it was truly time to watch him squirm.

"So, what did you do today?"

His eyes darted around the table; his hands reached for the sandwich. In seconds, after he took a huge bite out of it, his face was covered with pastrami, sauerkraut, Russian dressing. "Nothing much," he said, his mouth full.

Nothing much. Just "visited" my ex-fiancée, dropped by her house, was up to no good.

"No really," I said, sipping my Diet Coke, staring at him unrelentingly. "What did you do?"

He chewed desperately. "I don't know. Drove around, mostly."

"Really. Where?"

"Oh, just around. Nowhere really. Here and there."

Here and there.

I had a fleeting fantasy of catching him off guard: I would tell him that I'd seen him at Adrienne's, demand an explanation. Then I would throw something (a matzo ball; a stuffed cabbage roll; a pickle) at his head, leave the restaurant; my dignity and self-respect intact. But when I imagined the moment that his face would fall, his voice crack—the moment when he would say all the things I dreaded most (*You're right. I'm so sorry. . . . Adrienne and I still have feelings for each other. . . . I don't think I can go through with the wedding. . . . It's probably for the best. . . . I never ever meant to hurt you*), when he would tell me, finally, as I always feared he would, that he was leaving me for her—I realized suddenly that I was entirely unprepared. Though nothing at all had happened yet—I had said nothing; he had said nothing; I didn't even know, really, what (if anything) was going on between them—I felt stricken. Everything was quiet; the air was thin; I could barely breathe.

Outside the bubble of my doomsday scenario, life went on: conversation continued, silverware scraped against plates. Gayle and Donald talked, ate, wiped their mouths with napkins. Minutes passed. The check came; Donald paid it. They stood, put on their coats, stared at me, still sitting, not moving.

"Honey?" Donald said.

I swallowed.

The dangerous moment had passed.

Disaster had been (temporarily) averted; life remained (temporarily) unaltered. Had I not scared myself silly, I would have wept.

Donald put his arm around me; walked me to my car; folded me into it. Gayle walked on the other side of Donald, who insisted on taking Gayle back to Georgetown. I should go straight home, he said; he'd return in fifteen minutes.

But by the time he arrived, I was in bed, overcome by the kind of fatigue deep fear and panic leave behind. I stripped off my clothes; crawled under the covers. I couldn't face myself; Donald; what I had done; where he had been; what we each might say.

23

I slept fitfully; awoke after nine in the morning completely exhausted. Donald had left for work by then, and there was a note on the night table beside me. For a second or two I hesitated: *Could it be . . . ?* But it wasn't. Just a few harmless lines telling me he was sorry about the fight we'd had the day before, and that he looked forward to having dinner with me that evening.

I rolled over; burrowed my head into the pillows; tried to figure out why I felt so lousy. And then it came to me:

I felt hung over.

In the aftermath of the previous day's activities (surveillance, surveillance, surveillance) and excesses (fear, anxiety, suspiciousness, paranoia), I was tense. And something else, too—in need of a fix:

Hair of the dog.

I dressed quickly, brushed my teeth, tucked my hair up into one of Donald's old Mets caps, and headed out to my car. In the coming weeks, the inside of my Jetta, with its double cup-holders, its reclining front seats, its ample glove compartment, adjustable visors and mirrors and headrests, quick-accelerating V-6 engine, would become the control center for all my spying activities. I would live in that car; cry in that car; contemplate my future (or, as it seemed more and more, lack thereof) in that car. From the driver's seat—with my small measure of control and power behind the wheel—I carried out my mission: to get to the bottom of what was going on with Donald and Adrienne.

It goes without saying, of course, that had I still been in the care of Dr. Frond, or, for that matter, any reputable mental heath care professional, I would have had a slightly different mission: I would have been trying to get to the bottom of what was going on with *me*—my suspicions, my paranoia, my extreme lack of trust in

Donald, in our relationship. But I was not in the care of anyone. Free to roam the streets, my thoughts unbridled, I was a disaster waiting to happen.

And so that morning it began, the obsessive-compulsive routine that was, now, officially, taking over my life. After a quick stop for coffee at the bookstore, I would get back in the car, put my cap, scarf and sunglasses on, and commence to drive by.

What I thought I might find driving by her house in the morning, late morning, then noon, two, four, and five-thirty—and then past the parking lot at the Sidwell Friends School to finish the loop—I do not know. Maybe I was looking for inconsistencies (a late start or a sudden day off for Adrienne; the absence all week of Terrance's car parked in front of her house); certainly I was looking for outright flagrancies (any evidence of Donald and Adrienne sneaking off for lunchtime escapades; after-work sexcapades).

Round and round I would go through the neighborhood in my car, making my little boxes, my eyes glued to the window, assessing the scenes I had just seen. Round and round. A crazy person with a head full of misfiring, misdirected, mistrustful impulses.

Mind you, I still somehow managed to maintain the illusion of a (semi-)normal life being lived in between the drive-bys. I'd work for a few hours in the morning—*Fat to Fit* still hadn't gone away, thanks to its ongoing subtitle problems, and I was up to my ears in the author's recent pile of tardily delivered pseudo-scientificized charts ("How Fat Are You?"; "How Fit Do You Want to Become?"), graphs ("How Fat Most People Are"; "How Fit Most People Should Be"), and illustrated exercise instructions (*"fig. 1:* Buttocks up"; *"fig. 2:* Buttocks down"; *"fig. 3:* Buttocks tight"; *"fig. 4:* Buttocks relaxed").

Right.

Then, I'd run errands, go to the post office, cleaner's, pick up food for dinner. I'd make calls from the house to wedding vendors;

or on my cell phone to Gayle, or to Donald's voicemail at school to check in, say hello. But soon even these obligatory normalcies turned into excuses for more surveillance: after stopping inside quickly and checking my email, I would check Donald's; after going through that day's pile of magazines and mail, I would go through Donald's desk; after making the bed, I would examine all of Donald's clothes, check the pockets for receipts, inspect the collars for lipstick, sniff for Annick Goutal.

In the evenings, the routine, though slightly altered, continued. I would tell Donald I was taking a class, or going to a bookstore reading, or meeting Gayle for a drink or for dinner, or in need of (yet another) trip to Neiman's to inspect their (potential wedding) shoe selection. Then I would jump in the car, don my cap and scarf, readjust the visors and mirrors, and drive off into the evening up Connecticut toward Morrison Street. Only now that Adrienne would be, could be, home from work, I had to be more careful not to be seen.

Some nights on those surveillance excursions, I would find her car parked, as expected, in front of her house; sometimes Terrance's white Subaru wagon, too. And when I did, I would drive past a second time, sometimes a third time, to assess the situation, get an accurate picture of what she was doing (once, for example, I saw her through the window on the left side of the house, standing in the kitchen, by the sink; another time she and Terrance were clearly visible, talking, through the living room windows). Then, I would park down the street under that huge oak tree and wait for something to happen, checking my rearview and side mirrors almost constantly, for some sort of activity.

Occasionally, my vigilance and patience (unmitigated madness) would be rewarded: I would see her, still in her work clothes, taking files and books out of her car, a shopping bag out of the trunk. Or I might catch a glimpse of her slipping out the back door, having changed into jeans and a sweater, with an armful of newspapers for the recycling bin; or heading out in her tight black Lycra bodysuit for an evening run. Sometimes I would follow her through the streets as she ran, mapping her route; sometimes I would just wait in the car until she returned (I liked to make sure she returned before leaving my post for the night).

On the nights I drove by her house and her car wasn't there, I would cruise the neighborhood, a little frantically, looking for it (luckily, there weren't that many midnight-blue convertible Porsche Boxsters around, with National Gallery of Art parking permits and Yale University stickers, so it was fairly easy to spot). Once or twice I found it in the Safeway parking lot just around the corner from her house; another time I came upon it almost by accident parked down a side street near Politics and Prose (I'd assumed she was inside, attending a reading); I even spotted it in the parking garage of Mazza Gallerie, the nearby mall, when I was in truth going to Neiman's to inspect their shoe selection (I didn't go into the store that night, of course, but parked for a while on the opposite side of the parking level until I saw her go to her car, shopping bags in tow; then followed her home).

Several weeks passed; I found nothing of substance. But I remained unconvinced.

Donald, by this time, was getting suspicious himself. It seemed I'd been spending so much time spying on him and Adrienne that he'd started to wonder.

"You're never home anymore," he said plaintively one night. It was a cold evening in late February and he was sitting in the dining room, staring at a rotisserie chicken I'd picked up that morning at Fresh Fields. He'd set the table for two while I was upstairs; long white candles were even waiting in their silver holders to be lit. But I had my coat on and my keys in my hand, all ready to go out into the night.

"I'm always home," I said, huffing, puffing, with the kind of light sarcastic tone liars use when they're covering their tracks.

"No you're not. I mean, right now, for instance. You're on your way out. Again. If I'd come home five minutes later, I would have missed you."

I nodded, said nothing. He was right. I had the note I was going to leave for him ("See you around nine. Organic, free-range, politically correct chicken in the fridge") right there, in my pocket.

"So, where are you off to tonight?"

Tonight? I thought quickly, scanned the excuses I'd used over the past week. There had been the evening lecture series on the Human Genome Project at the Smithsonian that I'd said I'd been attending on Monday nights. The classics book club at Politics and Prose I'd said I'd been going to on Tuesday nights. Wednesday nights I usually used Gayle as a cover. Thursday and Friday evenings were swing nights (no set excuses; home from surveillance by seven-thirty at the latest, in time for dinner): necessitating a potpourri of miscellaneous unforeseen errands (shoe shopping, food shopping, video rentals and returns).

"Well, tonight," I started, slowly, trying to make it up as I went along. But I suddenly went blank. "What is tonight anyway?"

Donald's face fell. "It's Monday."

"Of course. Monday."

"The Smithsonian class, right?" he prompted.

"Right."

He looked at me, pushed the chicken away. "You're not taking a class at the Smithsonian, are you?"

I froze, completely flummoxed.

"Come on," he said, "tell me the truth. You're not taking a class, or going to some stupid book club at the bookstore, or doing any of the things you keep telling me you're doing every night."

"I'm not?" I was finally getting busted. He knew about my spying activities, my drive-bys, my bizarre behavior. It was all, finally, going to come crashing down.

"No. You're not."

"Then what am I doing?" I said. And I really did want to know. Somehow, I needed him to articulate and explain (as if anyone could, really) my self-generated self-destruction.

"You're having an affair," he said, matter-of-factly, as if he'd given it a great deal of painful thought. He smoothed the cloth napkin next to his plate back and forth with his hand. His face looked drawn and worried, and I realized that he'd lost weight.

Out of relief and glee at having been spared the humiliation of getting unmasked, I laughed out loud. "An affair!" More relief and glee; more nervous laughter. "Of course I'm not having an affair! What on earth would make you think that?"

"What on earth would make me think that? What on earth would make me think anything other than that? I mean, Elise, I barely ever see you anymore. You're never home. You're out every night, under extremely flimsy pretenses. When you are here you're distant. I feel like we're growing further and further apart every day." He stopped and shook his head. "I miss you. I miss talking to you. Complaining to you. Seeing your outrage on my behalf. I feel like you don't love me anymore."

He took his glasses off and set them down on the table, and for the first time I saw how troubled his eyes were, how sad. For a moment, I was unable to breathe. I missed him terribly, suddenly; wished I could run to him, hold onto him for dear life; stop the madness I was perpetuating. But I couldn't, because the other crazy part of me wanted to lash out and accuse *him* of having an affair, of falling out of love with me and in love with Adrienne. I clammed up. Hurling those sorts of accusations would only make him deny them; if I tried to back them up with bits and pieces from my spying expeditions, I would expose myself as the lunatic fiancée he was absolutely justified in jilting. My head swam; my mouth went dry. I forced myself to say something.

"Of course I still love you," I said finally, barely a whisper. "I've just been—I'm under a lot of stress right now, you know, with the wedding, with everything. Getting out at night, having activities," I lied, "it distracts me, clears my head."

He nodded, thought about what I had said. "Elise. Listen. You're not still worried about Adrienne, are you?"

I huffed, puffed, rolled my eyes. Of course I wasn't still worried about Adrienne. I was just tailing her twenty-four hours a day.

"Because there's nothing to worry about there. She and I are just friends. Absolutely nothing more. You know that."

Did I?

"Well, if you don't, you should."

Donald stepped toward me, put his arms around me, held me tight. Then he reached down and kissed me. I looked up, blinked backed tears I felt could give me away. I wanted suddenly to come clean, to admit my fears and suspicions, my unconscionably bad behavior. Like a fugitive spy, I wanted to come in from the cold.

But holding on to Donald, inhaling the smell of his freshly laundered T-shirt, I knew I couldn't.

Not just yet.

24

But when I finally came upon them, Donald and Adrienne, it was almost by accident: by that I mean, for once, I wasn't snooping, but merely out, driving, with no ulterior motive. Dr. Frond, of course, would have had a moment of silence: to her, nothing—not the alignment of the planets; not the seeming randomness of two people (or, in this case, three) being in the same place at the same time—was an accident. I must have made it happen.

I was heading up Wisconsin Avenue, about to make a left and go down Albemarle to the Crate and Barrel on Massachusetts Avenue (the store had called; there was a "slight problem" with our online bridal registry: They'd lost it). What was remarkable that Friday morning was that my intended route to Crate and Barrel could have easily and with absolute legitimacy taken me past both the Sidwell Friends school and Adrienne's street, where I could have knocked off two late-morning drive-bys. But for some inexplicable reason—Donald's lingering sadness from the night before, and my inability to talk myself back into sanity and stay home and have dinner with him—that day I had decided to forgo those drive-bys until later in the afternoon. Seeing them together on the street, walking slowly toward Donald's car, hit me like an express train.

Even though I was driving, I felt my knees buckle. Trying not to veer into oncoming traffic, I watched them, walking, talking, as if in the same silent underwater pantomime that I'd observed weeks before in front of Adrienne's house. I pulled over at the first opportunity, then looked out the window again. They were now getting into Donald's car; a few seconds later the car headed up Wisconsin.

I jammed the stick shift into first and pulled out after them, trying my best to keep a safe distance so they wouldn't see me. Up they went past Neiman's, then a right onto Western Avenue, straight through to Chevy Chase Circle and down two blocks, to the left-turn lane at Morrison Street. The morning rush-hour traffic had long since thinned; only the nannies were out now, pushing strollers through the tree-lined neighborhood. I pulled over again, let them make their turn, then made my way to the turn and went slowly down Morrison, too, stopping well before Adrienne's house. Crawling down the right shoulder of her street, I pulled up behind a line of parked cars where I knew they couldn't see me. Donald had parked in front of the house; he and Adrienne were walking slowly across the lawn, up the stairs, then inside.

The door closed behind them.

My eyes checked the dashboard clock: eleven forty-five. Donald should have been in school (in between his ninth-grade English section and his tenth-grade section). Adrienne should have been at work.

I thought and thought, but I couldn't make sense of it. Clearly, Donald had lied to me—twice now—about seeing Adrienne on the sly. But if this were a romantic tryst, why a Friday morning? And what was over on that part of Wisconsin Avenue?

Without taking my eyes off her house, I rooted around in my bag for my phone. When I found it I flipped it open and speed-dialed Gayle at *Congressional Quarterly*. Voicemail. I hung up without leaving a message. I tried to think of whom else to call, but the obvious choices seemed like bad ones. Fran would say I was an asswipe, tell me she'd told me so; Anne would wash her hands of me once and for all and never give me any more work.

I glanced at the clock again: five past twelve.

Suddenly, the front door opened, Donald walked quickly to his car, got behind the wheel, drove down Morrison to make a half-box via Livingston Street out to Connecticut. Instead of following him, I made a U-turn, then headed back toward Connecticut, just in time to see his car edging out into traffic. He crossed over, headed further down Livingston toward Reno Road. Following him there and then over to Wisconsin, I knew he was going back to school. From across the street I watched him pull into the Sidwell teachers' lot, park, then run across the pavement— the wind blowing his navy-blue blazer open and his tie over his shoulder—up the lawn to the door of the Upper School.

I returned home, sat in the living room, did nothing. The rest of the day was shot.

When Donald came home from school at five o'clock, slightly subdued but still, somewhat, his usual self, I tried to pretend that nothing was wrong; that I hadn't, earlier that day, espied my fiancé, yet again, up to no good, seeing his ex-fiancée on the sly. We ate some mediocre take-out (Indian) and watched a video (*The Third Man*) that I'd rented during one of my middle-of-the-week drive-by justification excuses; went to bed early. Neither of us, as luck would have it, seemed to feel like talking.

The following afternoon, Saturday, after Donald went to the gym (I knew he actually went to the gym because, of course, I followed him there), alone (I knew Adrienne wasn't meeting him there because after following Donald to the gym I drove by her house and saw her car there), I did a complete sweeping search of the premises: Donald's email, home voicemail, date book, desk drawers, dresser drawers, pants pockets, coat pockets.

Nothing.

Confounded, I paced the house: there was something I was missing; something I had overlooked.

But before I could figure out what that was, the phone rang. I turned to answer it and realized midway into the second ring that it wasn't the desk phone but rather Donald's cell phone, which, in his haste to get to the gym (to burn off those alleged love handles), he'd left behind, somewhere in his study. Tracking the ringing, I followed the sound to its source: the pocket of his navy-blue blazer that was hanging on the back of his desk chair. I flipped it open, stared at the green glowing LCD Caller ID panel:

Adrienne Adler, 202/555-2939.

Her home number.

It rang and rang—seven or eight times in all, I think. And though I was dying to answer it—dying to catch her red-handed—I waited for the call to go through to his voicemail. Breathing breathing breathing, I waited another minute or two for her to leave her message. Then I pounced on the phone as if it were a live mouse.

I hit the automatic voicemail retrieval button, waited as it connected.

"Donald. It's Adrienne, on Saturday, just after three o'clock. I thought I should call you the minute I heard. I got the test results back, and it's positive. Obviously we need to talk about this, as soon as possible, to figure out what we're going to do. If you can see your way clear to get away later on and come by, I'll be here for the rest of the day."

My heart beating wildly, I fell into Donald's desk chair and slumped forward.

The test results were positive.

Obviously they needed to talk about this as soon as possible. To figure out what they were going to do.

Her voice sounded trembly—genuinely scared. I reached for the real phone to call Gayle. But my hand was shaking too violently to dial, and I realized suddenly that I was too devastated to speak.

Adrienne was pregnant.

Donald was the father.

Any minute now—tonight, tomorrow, the day after that—he would tell me that Adrienne was a different person, a new woman, that she'd changed her mind about not wanting children and that he was leaving me to marry her and have their baby.

The situation seemed somehow unreal: despite myself, I had believed in Donald. I had loved him deeply and believed that he had loved me. For all my doubt and distrust, I had never truly thought that any of my suspicions would ever be confirmed.

I walked the floors of the house like a ghost; floating from room to room, silently, touching nothing, barely breathing. An hour must have passed; maybe two—it was already starting to get dark when Donald called, from a pay phone at the gym. I let his call go through to voicemail, too, and then I listened to it: he'd retrieved a message off his cell phone and had to take care of something unexpectedly. He'd be at least a few hours; he'd check in with me later and let me know when he might be home.

Might be home.

Eventually, my hand steadied; I called Gayle, told her the news.

"But what makes you so sure they will actually have the baby? I mean, maybe they won't. Didn't Donald tell you that Adrienne didn't want children? Maybe she'll have an abortion. Donald would then beg your forgiveness, and things between you could go back to normal."

I didn't answer. Things could never go back to normal.

"Listen," she started, but before she could get out whatever harebrained plan she had instantly come up with, I cut her off. My bile was rising; shock and devastation were giving way to hatred and rage. It was my turn to call the shots here. But then I found that I was crying.

"No, *you* listen. We're going over there together, you and me, and I'm going to end this charade once and for all. I'm going to expose them, let them know that I know their little secret before they can blindside me with it."

Gayle was silent; nervous, I knew. I'm not sure she had ever known me to cry before.

"That woman's ruined my life, Gayle. She's done what she came here to do: break us up, get Donald back. She set her trap and snared her prey. And she did it using the oldest trick in the book—getting pregnant." I tried to collect myself. "Considering what's happened, I deserve a small measure of satisfaction. I deserve to be left with at least the merest shred of dignity. If I go there and tell them I know before they drop the bomb on me, I won't look like a complete idiot."

Gayle offered in a soft, soft voice to pick me up. Given my emotional and physical state, that sounded like a good idea. And so, twenty minutes later, just after six o'clock, my eyes dry and my face pale, I left the house and ran across the lawn in the dark to her car.

25

"Listen," Gayle said, swerving through the dark quiet streets of northwest Washington (she was a terrible driver). "I hope you don't mind, but I took the liberty of calling Fran."

"To do what? Come with us?" I couldn't even begin to imagine what that would be like.

"No no no." She jerked the car to the right; narrowly avoided a jogger and two pedestrians carrying Safeway bags. "Just to extract her moral support."

"And?" I was almost afraid to hear what Fran had said.

"And, well, she was absolutely one hundred percent on your side and completely disgusted with Adrienne. Called her a 'skank' and a 'slut' and something else rather—"

"Okay. I get the picture."

"Really, she was terribly sorry for ever having taken to her in the first place. As am I, of course. We were tricked and seduced, you see."

"Fran? Terribly sorry for anything? I don't believe it."

She turned to face me in an attempt to convince me how completely true her tale of Fran's contrition was. But I didn't buy it for an instant. And besides, I couldn't concentrate on anything. Not only was Gayle a menace behind the wheel, but I was a terrible passenger—seeing death and disfigurement around every corner.

I pushed my hand up against the dashboard, melodramatically. "Watch the road."

"Yes."

"No really. I mean, watch it. I don't want to get into an accident right now. I'm not in the mood."

"Yes."

Glancing around at her, I saw a bit of collar peeking out of her coat. "You're still wearing that stupid Linda Hunt shirt. I thought we talked about that."

"Yes."

"Yes what?"

"Yes I'll get rid of it. I promise."

Maybe I was wrong about the shirt—maybe it wasn't so bad—I didn't know anything anymore. Except this: We were almost there.

Gayle made the right onto Morrison Street, and, having trained at the hands of one of the great all-time masters of the surveillance drive-by, immediately slowed down, cut the lights. I was deeply grateful for her technical competence. Not to mention her moral support and understanding. I was in desperate need of it now.

On the initial approach to the house, we saw Donald's car, as expected, parked out front. And even though it was not a surprise, even though I knew with absolute certainty that he was there, that we would find him there, it was still a shock. Neither my mind nor my body had gotten used to the idea that he was, and had been, for God knows how long, cheating on me with her. And I didn't know if it ever would.

Instead of going past the house this time and parking under the big oak tree, we pulled in just before it, behind a giant four-wheel-drive Expedition (or Excursion, or Escalade, or Escapade) SUV that provided us excellent cover. Gayle shut the engine off, then reached behind her to the back seat.

"I wasn't sure how long we would be here, so I packed a little snack in case we get hungry."

Out of the bag came bottled water, apples, Ziploc baggies filled with cheese slices, expensive crackers, Swiss chocolate.

"Unless there's a pair of night-vision binoculars in there, I'm not interested," I said.

"Can you see anything?" Gayle asked.

I suddenly saw movement into the living room—silhouetted figures, which were clearly Donald and Adrienne, behind the thin sheer curtains.

"Okay. They're in there. In the living room."

Gayle's hands clutched the Ziploc baggies of food tightly.

I craned my neck, contorting myself in the front seat against the dashboard and the curved windshield. "But I can't see what they're doing."

"They're probably talking."

They certainly had a *lot* to talk about. I scanned the house, tried to figure out if there was a way I could go out there, hide in the front just below the living room windows, peek and listen, but the azalea bushes were too low, too sparsely planted. Unlike the giant SUV, they would never cover me. Then I noticed the left side of the house, toward the back, where the kitchen was. Big bushes. Thick and dense and just the right height.

It didn't take long before they went into the kitchen; maybe fifteen minutes. Excitedly, I grabbed Gayle's arm. "They're moving. They're moving," I announced, like some overzealous Secret Service agent. I could see them fairly clearly now through the bare windows—Adrienne in a dark pullover sweater and jeans, her hair up in a clip; Donald wearing the same clothes he'd left with earlier in the day, also a dark sweater and jeans. She leaned against the counter, with her back to the sink; he stood beside the refrigerator, then sat down at the kitchen table that was right by the windows.

It was like watching a silent movie.

Adrienne left the room momentarily, went into the living room, took something off the bookshelves, and returned to the kitchen. She sat down at the table next to Donald. They appeared to be talking. But I couldn't see what they were doing. What any of it meant.

"I'm going in," I announced suddenly, sounding even more ridiculously officious, like a Navy SEAL.

Gayle dropped the baggies onto her lap. "You can't be serious! We'll be caught for peeping!"

"I'm serious. I'm going to find out what the hell is going on."

Before she could stop me, I zipped my jacket up, slid out of the car, pushed the door silently closed, and ran quickly past the giant SUV. Crouching, the way detectives do on television, I ran up the stretch of grass to the row of bushes just under the kitchen window. I was terrified but excited.

It was dark and very quiet there in the bushes, and though it was quite chilly, I noticed I was sweating. I unzipped my jacket, wiped my forehead, my cheeks, with my open hand. Then I closed my eyes, waited for my breathing to slow, my pulse to stop pounding in my ears, so I could hear again. Finally, through the window, through the glass that was open just a crack, I heard them:

"Look," Adrienne said. "Remember this? That time we went to Martha's Vineyard."

A pause.

"Wow," Donald said, wistfully. "Look how young we looked. How small Lucy was. How thin I was."

"And look. At these. That week in the Hamptons, Saga-ponack."

Another pause.

"It feels like a hundred years ago, doesn't it?" she said.

"More. It feels like a thousand years ago."

They were looking through photo albums, obviously. Reminiscing about their past. Clearing the way for their future. Their baby. I tried to wrap my mind around the finality of it all, the deep anger I felt; the deep sadness I knew would soon follow. *Donald had deceived me; been unfaithful to me. Our life together was completely over. Their years of history, sustained connection, had in the end won out.*

I could see the tops of their heads as they sat, side by side, hunched over at the table. I looked up into the sky—cloudless, and the color of slate—and felt my eyes burn with tears. After weeks of fruitless searches, stakeouts, drive-bys, my deepest darkest fears had been confirmed.

The familiar piercing ring of a cell phone went off. I jumped. My eyes darted to the kitchen window and saw Donald and Adrienne both sit up, patting themselves. Realizing it was neither of theirs, they looked at each other. Then both turned to look out the window.

Suddenly aware that it was my cell phone that was ringing and desperate to make it stop, I crouched down, crawled away from the house toward the driveway, reached into my jacket and flipped open my phone.

The Caller ID box lit up: it was Gayle.

Calling from the car, from her cell phone, eager to find out what was going on.

Before I could run, or hide, or otherwise disappear into the night, I heard the back screen door slam and feet running down the stairs. Donald appeared, looming over me, his face stern and half in shadow. Adrienne was just behind him. I felt paralyzed with dread.

He stared at me, his eyes cold, his mouth open. "What are you doing here?"

I stood up and stared back, unable to speak.

"Were you following me?"

Silence.

"Spying on us?" He looked up at the window, and the bushes, and back at Adrienne, incredulous. She crossed her arms, looked down, and didn't say anything. Then they both stood there, waiting for an answer.

I didn't have one.

"Were you out here lurking and listening and—?" He was having a hard time finishing the sentence; he simply could not comprehend what had driven me to do what he was slowly realizing I'd done. His eyes widened, and the veins in his neck grew visible. "Jesus Christ, Elise. What are you, crazy?" '

"You've misunderstood this whole thing," Adrienne said to me, an enigmatic smile on her lips.

I continued to stare, say nothing.

"Why are you doing this?" Donald went on. "Why, on earth, would you follow me like a criminal, when I've given you absolutely no reason to do so?"

"*No reason?*" I replied at last. "How can you say that? There've been plenty of reasons. I mean, look where you are right now. Here. At Adrienne's. Sneaking around behind my back." I put my hands on my hips. "And where were you yesterday? Around lunchtime? When you were supposed to be in school? And she," I said, glancing over at Adrienne, but not deigning to address her directly, "was supposed to be at work?"

"Really, Elise," her voice was thick with condescension. "You've misread *everything*."

He looked furious, turned his head. "Shut up, Adrienne."

I was on a roll. I'd caught him completely off guard and he was nervous.

"And a few weeks ago," I continued. "After we had that fight. You came over here. I saw your car. I know what you've been doing."

"You know what I've been doing," he said, his voice flat.

"Yes, Donald," I said firmly. "I know what you've been doing. What the two of you have been doing." I took a breath, created a space for the precise moment to drop my bomb: "I know about the baby."

A second or two passed; Donald's face, instead of becoming more enraged, simply looked confused. His brow furrowed. "*Baby?*" he said.

"Listen, Donald. I heard the message Adrienne left you today, on your cell phone. About the test results being positive. I know the two of you have been seeing each other, and that now you're . . ." I took a step back, regarding them both from a distance. "Now she's pregnant, and I don't know when, if ever, you were planning on telling me." I stared only at him. "I just can't believe you would do this to me."

There was an expression on Donald's face that I'd never seen before: it was as if I were a stranger to him; someone he didn't know; someone he didn't particularly like.

"Adrienne's not pregnant," he said.

"*Really*. Then why did her test results come back 'positive'?"

I had him. I knew I had him.

"The test results weren't hers," he said slowly, his face pained. "They were Lucy's."

I blinked.

"Lucy has cancer. In her leg and behind her eye. She's dying."

I blinked again.

"She got sick a few weeks ago, out of the blue—that day, after our fight. Yesterday when you saw us together we had taken her to the veterinary hospital for tests. Today, this afternoon, we got the results back. Adrienne called to tell me that. And I came over here because we had to make a decision. Which is what we've been doing since I got here."

All the blood seemed to drain from my body. I looked from Donald to Adrienne, wondering, for a split second, if she had orchestrated this whole thing—lied about the dog's ailments and dire test results—in order to get him back. But when I looked at Donald again, I realized it was all true: Lucy really was sick; he had been heartsick because of it; he had been spending time here to deal with the situation because I wasn't there for him.

"Why didn't you just tell me?" I whispered. I was trying desperately not to panic: I knew I had wounded Donald to the core.

"Because I knew how you felt about Lucy; about Adrienne;

how jealous you were of them, of their place in my past. I knew it would make you mad if I needed to spend time here, with both of them, until it was over. I knew you wouldn't understand."

I nodded. He was right. I wouldn't have understood.

"Lucy was with me during some very difficult times, some very important times in my life. My breakup with Adrienne; my move from New York; the years here when I was trying to start over; when I met you. She stood by me; trusted me completely; asked for almost nothing in return." He stopped a minute, stood completely still. "I just can't believe she won't be around anymore; that we're going to have to put her down."

"I'm sorry," I whispered. And I was. About everything. "But you can understand why I came to the conclusions I came to," I said to Donald. "You can see why I might have misunderstood what was going on. Can't you?"

He looked at Adrienne harshly, with what seemed like new eyes. "I can see how Adrienne didn't help things by moving here at such a difficult time for us and fueling your suspicions. She's never been one to just fade into the background and not cause trouble." For a second I felt one sharp pang of satisfaction: Donald had, at this late point at least, seen her culpability; acknowledged that she wasn't innocent in all this.

Then he turned to me. I looked away quickly, too ashamed to meet his eye. "But I thought you knew me," he said. "I thought you knew me better than that." He dropped his head. "And I thought I knew you better than that. Only you've turned into exactly what I didn't want: someone I can't talk to." Then he walked slowly back to the house and up the stairs.

Adrienne glared at me before she turned and went inside. Donald had found her out and shamed her, too, which she clearly hadn't expected and didn't like. The look on her face withered me. I was no better than she was.

Alone on the grass, before Gayle materialized, took my hand, led me back to the car, I stood. The air was cold and damp; the night suddenly, completely silent. For a moment or two the world was so still it seemed to have disappeared.

So this is what it feels like when the universe collapses, I thought.

26

I've thought about that night many times in the months since it happened: thought about faith and uncertainty; about love and jealousy; about what it means when you stop trusting someone you love, or when they stop trusting you. The bottom drops out; the center does not hold. Love is a mirage, an inkblot, subject to position, mood, interpretation. Relative, changeable, unstable, it can appear—or disappear—at any moment.

At least, that's what I used to think.

The night I watched Donald turn away from me and go back into Adrienne's house, I believed, with complete certainty, that I had seen the last of him; that the wedding was off; that he would never, ever come home. And who could have blamed him? What I'd done, how I'd behaved, was unforgivable. I had, without a doubt, destroyed us; sucked every last bit of joy and happiness and trust and love out of him. I had seen things that weren't there; ignored things that were. I had driven him away. The Evil Twins had worked their evil magic, I had given in to my darkest fears, and, because I couldn't help myself, the person most precious to me in the whole wide world was gone forever.

But Donald wasn't like me; didn't think like me; didn't act like me. Love, to him, was not a mirage or an inkblot; it was not relative, changeable, unstable. Despite my abominably bad behavior, my terrible lack of trust in him, he came home two nights later, crawled into bed beside me, and fell asleep. And though he barely spoke to me over the course of the following week—barely said a word, spoke a sentence, unless it was absolutely essential ("Hi," "Hello," "Good night," "I'll see you later," "I won't be home for dinner")—he stayed; did not abandon ship.

I don't know why he did that.

I have no idea what he told himself to explain my behavior; what excuses he made to himself for deciding to stay with someone as crazy as me.

Maybe he'd chosen to look at what I'd done—my spying, my surveillance, my jumping to all the wrong conclusions—in a positive light; as evidence of my strong feelings for him, my fear of losing him, my not wanting to live without him.

Or maybe he'd simply chosen to accept what I'd done, my all-too-human foibles, and move on.

Whatever it was, I thanked my lucky stars for it.

And for him.

That first week passed slowly. Donald and Adrienne drove the dog out to an animal hospital in Germantown, and there, on a freezing night in late February, they had her put to sleep. Watching her slip into that faraway permanent slumber, they wept; consoled each other.

When Donald returned home, he made no effort to hide his grief or excuse it. He looked sadder than I'd ever seen him look.

Days melted into weeks, and ever so slowly, our lives went back to pretty much the way they had been before my psychotic break. Donald went to school with the usual bags of chocolate; obsessed about his weight; prepared his lessons with grave attentiveness; used the StairMaster to the brink of exhaustion. I spent a lot of time with Gayle, trying to apologize and make up for my months of inexcusable self-centeredness; had coffee with Fran a few times at the store; drove through the back streets of our neighborhood, into Rock Creek Park, and down around all the monuments.

Sometimes, in the afternoon, I would park my car near the Kennedy Center, then walk down to the Lincoln Memorial and over the bridge into Virginia, feeling the early spring wind against my face and watching the tourists streaming back from Arlington National Cemetery. Once in a while, in the evening, I would drive down to the Jefferson Memorial, or the FDR Memorial, or the Vietnam Veterans Memorial—all lit up and bathed in a yellow-white glow—and sit in the car with all the windows rolled down, thinking. Thinking about what I had, and what I'd almost lost, and how narrow my world had gotten. After a while, I started thinking about other things, too. Things I'd all but stopped thinking about during the Age of Adrienne: real books; movies; the present; the future; the world.

In early March, just as the trees were starting to bud again and turn green, I made a trip to New York to reconnect with Anne. It had been a while—too long, really—and we had a lot of catching up (gossiping) to do. *Fat to Fit* was finally finished and ready to go to the printer, with its new, harmlessly unambiguous, and completely forgettable subtitle: *How to Transform Your Body—and Your Mind—in Only Ten Weeks*; but a book I'd worked on the year before, *How to Stay Married Forever,* was having its publication delayed indefinitely: its author, Anne reported over lunch at her desk (a giant Diet Coke and six Marlboro Lights for her; a heavenly tuna sandwich on rye for me), was recently "outed" by *New York* magazine as having been divorced twice.

I returned home to Washington later that same day, with a manuscript only a mother could love: *Not the Same Old Story: Coping with Perimenopause.* Flipping through it at my desk, I could have hugged it. But I knew, too, that I could not do this work much longer. The next morning I enrolled for the summer graduate session at Georgetown and looked toward the months ahead. Only ten more credits to go before a completely new phase of my life—teaching—would begin, but a lot of self-reflection separated me from the job I wanted next.

Though Adrienne didn't disappear completely from our lives, she did recede. Now that the strongest link between her and Donald had been broken—Lucy—there was little to connect them to each other. There were no more phone calls; no more dinner dates; no more invitations to come to brunch. The pretense of friendship between the two of them, and the three of us, had finally dissolved.

Donald heard from Terrance that they had stopped seeing each other. It had ended badly, of course. Adrienne had dumped him unceremoniously, without apology, and with little explanation shortly after the denouement in her side yard. Francesco was back in the picture—assuming he was ever really out of it to begin with—and it wasn't long before we found out that she was leaving her job at the National Gallery and heading back to New York. With the dog gone and her attempts to interfere with Donald and me all but thwarted, it seemed there was no reason whatsoever for her to stay.

Pondering the news of her retreat, I think we all—Donald, Terrance, and I—breathed a collective sigh of relief. We were free of her, finally; free of her seductions, manipulations, complications— real or imagined—and the havoc she wreaked.

But I am still not free of the memory of her and of my maniacal behavior. Like an illness, it lingers unpleasantly in the flesh, in the bones, in the mind.

One day in mid-March when I was home, working at my desk, a package arrived, hand-delivered by a DHL courier. It was from Antwerp, Belgium, and I knew immediately that it was the wedding dress from Dries. Afraid to open the box, I brought it upstairs. I put it in the back of my closet, next to a stack of boxes filled with shoes I never wear anymore.

It's still there, in fact, the dress; still unopened. I never did have any use for it, even though Donald and I did get married, as planned, several weeks later. But instead of trying to fulfill Fran and Adrienne's aesthetic visions of the perfect, indescribable, nothing-else-quite-like-it-in-the-world kind of gown, I wore a simple white dress, off the shoulder, that I bought up the street, off the rack, at Neiman's. It was a perfect April day, and somehow it all went off without a hitch.

Sometimes I still get the urge to drive down Morrison Street; to go through Donald's pockets; to sit up late at night, looking at his sleeping face, searching for signs that he doesn't love me anymore, that he will leave me, that our life together is over.

But those are tics; involuntary outbursts of uncertainty and fear.

What the future holds, what lurks on the dark side of the mind, all that is mysterious and unknown and invisible to the naked eye—my naked eye—will forever cause me to twitch with dread. As Dr. Frond used to say, the need to control that which we can't is born out of fear. And I have enough fear to last a lifetime.

If I learned one thing, though, during my downfall with Adrienne, it's this:

That what happens will happen whether I am watching or not.

Maintaining a constant vigilant eye will not keep disaster from striking, or the plane from crashing; it will not keep Donald from straying or from leaving me for someone else. Disaster will strike or not strike; the plane will crash or not crash; Donald will leave me for someone else or stay with me forever. Love, trust, faith—they are not equipped with radar devices, sonar devices, night-vision devices, lifetime guarantees.

They are blind as bats.

But they are all we have.

ACKNOWLEDGMENTS

With gratitude to Bill Clegg, Robin Desser, Paul Sidey, Andy McKillop, Mark McCallum, Sue Freestone, Marisa Pagano, Wendy Law-Yone, Nancy Pearlstein, Marian Brown, Elaine Goldsmith-Thomas, and especially Jana Kollias, whose tales of pathology were truly inspirational.

A NOTE ABOUT THE AUTHOR

Laura Zigman spent ten years working in book publishing in New York. Her pieces have appeared in the *New York Times*, the *Washington Post*, and *USA Today*. She now lives outside Boston.

A NOTE ON THE TYPE

The text of this book was set in Electra, a typeface designed by W. A. Dwiggins (1880–1956). This face cannot be classified as either modern or old style. It is not based on any historical model, nor does it echo any particular period or style. It avoids the extreme contrasts between thick and thin elements that mark most modern faces, and it attempts to give a feeling of fluidity, power, and speed.

Composed by Creative Graphics,
Allentown, Pennsylvania

Printed and bound by Berryville Graphics,
Berryville, Virginia

Designed by Iris Weinstein